John Kenneth McLaughlin

The Best of
Five-Minute
Mysteries

The Best of
Five-Minute
Mysteries

Ken Weber

Stoddart

Published in 1999 by Stoddart Publishing Co. Limited
34 Lesmill Road, Toronto, Canada M3B 2T6

Distributed by:
General Distribution Services Ltd.
325 Humber College Blvd., Toronto, Canada M9W 7C3
Tel. (416) 213-1919   Fax (416) 213-1917
Email customer.service@ccmailgw.genpub.com

03   02   01   00   99   1   2   3   4   5

Canadian Cataloguing in Publication Data

Weber, K. J. (Kenneth Jerome), 1940-
The best of five-minute mysteries

ISBN 0-7737-3207-1

1. Detective and mystery stories, Canadian (English).*   2. Literary recreations.
3. Puzzles. I. Title

GV1507.D4W417 1999   793.73   C99-931452-1

Jacket Design: Bill Douglas @ The Bang
Text Design: Tannice Goddard

THE CANADA COUNCIL | LE CONSEIL DES ARTS
FOR THE ARTS | DU CANADA
SINCE 1957 | DEPUIS 1957

We acknowledge for their financial support of our publishing program the Canada Council, the Ontario Arts Council, and the Government of Canada through the Book Publishing Industry Development Program (BPIDP).

Printed and bound in Canada

For Cecile

CONTENTS

PREFACE   *XI*

1   THE PROWLER ON BURLEIGH COURT   *1*

2   DOUBLE SUICIDE ON MIDLAND RIDGE   *4*

3   A CLEVER SOLUTION AT THE COUNTY FAIR   *8*

4   A HOLDUP AT THE ADJALA BUILDING   *13*

5   A SURPRISE WITNESS FOR THE HIGHLAND PRESS CASE   *16*

6   THE CASE OF THE MISSING .38 SMITH AND WESSON   *20*

7   A 9-1-1 CALL FROM WHITBY TOWERS   *24*

8   BEFORE THE FIRST COMMERCIAL BREAK   *28*

9   TO CATCH A MANNERLY THIEF   *32*

10   SOMETHING SUSPICIOUS IN THE HARBOR   *37*

11   ESTY WILLS PREPARES FOR A BUSINESS TRIP   *40*

12   THE POWER OF CHANCE   *44*

13   AN UNLIKELY PLACE TO DIE   *48*

14   THE LAST WILL AND TESTAMENT OF NORVILLE DOBBS, ORTHOGRAPHER   *52*

15   NOT YOUR AVERAGE HARDWARE STORE   *55*

16   WHO HID THE MEDICINE?   *60*

17   SHOULD THE THIRD SECRETARY SIGN?   *64*

18   THE CASE OF THE JEWELRY THIEVES   *67*

19   THE MURDER OF MR. NORBERT GRAY   *71*

20 SOME UNCERTAINTY ABOUT THE CALL AT 291 BRISTOL *76*

21 THE CASE OF THE STOLEN STAMP COLLECTION *80*

22 THE CASE OF THE BUCKLE FILE *83*

23 A VERY BRIEF NON-INTERVIEW *88*

24 A CLEAN PLACE TO MAKE AN END OF IT *94*

25 MURDER AT THE DAVID WINKLER HOUSE *97*

26 A QUIET NIGHT WITH DANIELLE STEEL? *102*

27 RIGHT OVER THE EDGE OF OLD BALDY *106*

28 THE CASE OF QUEEN ISABELLA'S GIFT *109*

29 MURDER AT 249 HANOVER STREET *114*

30 WAITING OUT THE RAIN *118*

31 THE BODY ON BLANCHARD BEACH *123*

32 THE CASE OF THE MISSING CHILD *129*

33 THE CASE OF THE ATTEMPTED SUICIDE *134*

34 THE MISSION IN THE CLEARING *138*

35 IN SEARCH OF ANSWERS *144*

36 VANDALISM AT THE BEL MONTE GALLERY *149*

37 TWO SHOTS WERE FIRED *154*

38 INVESTIGATING THE FAILED DRUG BUST *159*

39 A DOUBLE ASSASSINATION AT "THE FALLS" *163*

40 A DECISION AT RATTLESNAKE POINT *167*

41	WHEN THE OXYGEN RAN OUT	172
42	THE CASE OF THE SCALPEL MURDER	177
43	SPY VERSUS SPY	181
44	THE CASE OF THE MISSING BODY	187
45	MORE THAN ONE ST. PLOUFFE?	191
46	NOTHING BETTER THAN A CLEAR ALIBI	196
47	THE SEARCH FOR OLIE JORGENSSON	200
48	WHILE LITTLE HARVEY WATCHED	204
49	A WITNESS IN THE PARK	208
50	DEATH IN THE BIDE-A-WEE MOTEL	212
	SOLUTIONS	219

PREFACE

▼

Like every novice, I began my first year as an English teacher
with a vision of myself charging the bastions of literary
insight, followed eagerly by troops of bright-eyed adoles-
cents. Then I met my first class.

"You'd be good for the 'opportunity class,'" my vice-
principle explained, " because . . . well . . . because you're
tall. Oh, don't worry about teaching them anything. Just try
to keep them busy. And off the furniture if you can. "

"Opportunity class" was the administration's vaguely
purposeful attempt to keep all its misfits in one, theoretically
manageable group, and it took this dubious cohort about a
minute to make clear to me that: a) they didn't read; and
b) they weren't particularly keen to remedy that situation.
My response turned out to be one of those inspirations we
are each granted a few times in life. For our next class, I
wrote and read aloud to them the five-minute mystery
that appears on page 80, "The Case of the Stolen Stamp
Collection" (in a much simpler version!).

The depth of their reaction confirmed two truths for me.
Everybody loves a good story. And (almost) everybody loves
to solve a mystery. Put these two ideas together and you have
a double pleasure. What I did not realize at the time was how
universal these truths are, for after the mysteries became a
regular "opportunity class" feature, other students began to

appear at my door — along with many of my colleagues — asking for copies to take home. The rest, as they say . . .

What follows in *The Best of Five-Minute Mysteries* is a far more sophisticated selection than I wrote in my teaching days, but like the early stories, these are all fun to read and, if you really try, fun to solve. As for "opportunity class" — did the students all become devoted readers? Well, yes and no. But they stayed off the furniture!

I hope you enjoy these.

Ken Weber

In the mysteries . . .

Easy: usually means that the solution is built around a single clue.

Moderate: in most cases, the solution involves putting together at least two pieces of information.

Challenge: usually requires some deduction after first extracting several pieces of information.

1

THE PROWLER ON BURLEIGH COURT

▼

C ode three meant he did not have to rush, but Sean
Dortmund put the red light on the roof anyway. He
didn't use the siren, however. There was no need at 3:00 AM.
Code Three meant gunfire with death or injury. It also meant
situation over, or well in hand so that officers responding
need not endanger themselves or the public getting to the
scene. But as inspector, Sean was the active ranking officer at
that time of the morning, and since the reports were eventually going to go out over his signature, he wanted to view the
scene himself.

The coroner's car, along with two black-and-whites and an
ambulance, had already filled the driveway by the time
Sean arrived, so he parked on the street. Burleigh Court
was a cul-de-sac with only six houses, all of them large and
custom-built. There was money here.

He was met on the sidewalk by two of the uniformed men, who took him past the yellow-tape barrier and into the house. "Everything's in place, Inspector. We got word you were coming." Detective Lalonde was waiting for him at the front hallway. "Victim is in there." He jerked his thumb toward an open door. "Here's the weapon." Lalonde held up a clear plastic bag with a revolver inside. "Three shots."

Sean could see three shell casings that looked to be .38 caliber.

"And the perp's in that room. We've got the story. Everything's clean. We're just waiting for you to give it a name: murder, manslaughter, self-defense or accident."

"Let's see the body first," Sean said, brushing past Lalonde and through the doorway to where the coroner, Jim Tait, was waiting for him.

"Meet the former Jean-Marc Lavaliere," Tait said grimly. He pulled back the sheet to reveal a very bloody corpse.

Sean leaned closer to compensate for the poor lighting. Lavaliere's body was lying on its back. He appeared to have been in his mid-thirties, athletic, and quite handsome. The track suit he wore looked brand-new. Sean crouched down and flicked several shards of glass off Lavaliere's chest for a better look at the wound. The window directly above had been smashed, and pieces of glass were spread all over this part of the room.

"Seems like he came in that way." Tait nodded at the broken window. "Anyway, she must have nailed him right away."

"She?" Sean looked up.

"Yeah," Tait said. "The perp. Ms. Dina White. You haven't spoken to her yet? I didn't realize."

Sean didn't say anything. He was known as a man of very few words so Tait just kept on talking.

"Anyway, they were partners, she and Lavaliere.

Advertising business. But according to her, things weren't going so well. Apparently he's a drinker, this guy — or was. They'd been having quite an argument over it for several weeks."

Sean just nodded.

"Anyway, he smashed the window to get in — I suppose we'll never know why. Maybe he was drunk. I'll autopsy that though. We'll know that by tomorrow. Anyway, she thought he was a prowler, and bingo! Three right in the chest. Suppose you can't blame her, really. A woman living alone. Your window gets smashed in at night . . . She must have been awful frightened."

Sean nodded again.

"Anyway, I can't move the remains here till you say so. Are you going to give it a name? Accident? Justifiable homicide?"

There was a long pause when Tait stopped, each man waiting for the other to speak.

"Homicide, yes," said Sean, breaking the silence, but just barely. He shook his head. "But not justifiable. No, I don't think so."

► *What has led Sean to suspect murder?*

2

DOUBLE SUICIDE ON
MIDLAND RIDGE

▼

E specially in the bright morning sun, the red Jeep wagon
seemed much too sporty a presence to be a suicide vehicle. It was a very shiny, metallic red, with roof rack and little
plastic streamers on the radio aerial, mud flaps behind all
four tires, and a gleaming chrome trailer hitch. The total
effect said sportsperson. Or camper or hiker. Someone in love
with life and adventure. Yet some time in the past few hours,
the Jeep had served an entirely opposite purpose.

From where he stood on a knoll just behind it, Francis
Cremer could see one of the bodies slumped over the steering
wheel. There was another, he knew; the patrolman had said
"a couple." Lovers, probably. Young people often spent the
evening hours here on Midland Ridge. It was a popular
place to park: private, romantic, and just far enough away
from town. Cremer walked down to the Jeep, where several

policemen were waiting for him. The ambulance attendants, fully aware now that any emergency had long since passed, had turned off their flashing lights and were leaning against their vehicles.

"Nothing has been touched, sir. "The youngest policeman was speaking to Cremer. "I've been here since we called you."

Cremer nodded. "You've got pictures of this?" He had put his fingers around the piece of vacuum-cleaner hose that ran from the exhaust pipe of the Jeep through a hole in the back window.

"Yeah, we got lots of shots, Frank." It was Zerlow, the senior uniformed man present and an acquaintance of Cremer's. "Do you want to know what angles?"

"Not now," Cremer replied. "It looks like a pretty straight-forward suicide. We probably won't even need what you have."

He worked loose a piece of masking tape from the edge of the back window with his thumbnail and peeled off a long strip.

"They must have used a whole roll of this stuff," he commented, mostly to himself, as he ran his fingers over the tape that covered the edges of the hole where the hose fed into the window. All the windows were taped as well; so much had been used where the hose met the exhaust pipe that it appeared as though someone had joined the two with a baseball.

Zerlow spoke again. "Pentland here found them at first light." He nodded at the young policeman. "We called the wagon first." This time he nodded at the ambulance. "But then it was pretty obvious that this was your bailiwick, So you were next. Nothing else has been done yet. Oh, except the license check." He took out a little notepad. "Vehicle's owned by one Owen P. Riggio, 219A First Avenue. That's probably him there."

Francis Cremer made himself look inside the Jeep. Almost thirty years as an investigator for the county coroner's office had not hardened him to death even a little. The man slumped over the steering wheel was likely in his mid-thirties, Cremer thought. He forced himself to look closer. Whether or not the man was Owen P. Riggio, he certainly appeared to have died from carbon-monoxide poisoning. The cherry-red lips suggested that. The other body was that of a woman. Cremer could see her light blonde hair, but couldn't see her face or lips because her body had slumped off the passenger seat and partially onto the floor, where it leaned awkwardly against the door. He suspected her lips, too, would be cherry red.

He picked at the end of a strip of masking tape on the driver's door until he had loosened a corner, then began to peel off the strip that covered the crack between the door and the frame.

"Do the tape on the passenger side, please, Zerlow," Francis Cremer said. "But don't open the door, she'll fall out. We'll work from this side."

Zerlow went to do his part; Cremer opened the driver's door very carefully. The silence of the death inside seemed to affect everything on the outside too. No one talked, or even coughed. The birds seemed to have disappeared. A cloud momentarily blocked the sun, making the scene even more tense.

"There's a note beside the gearshift!" Zerlow announced, breaking the spell. All the policemen, the ambulance attendants, and even Cremer began to breathe more slowly. One of the policemen came over for a closer look.

"I didn't see that, sir." The young one again.

"It doesn't matter," Cremer told him. "They were dead anyway."

He took a small leather case out of his inside jacket pocket, unzipped it, and extracted a tweezer. He handed the case to the policeman and, holding his breath, reached over the dead man to pull out the note.

"Come here," he said to Zerlow. "Look at this." Zerlow came around to the driver's side, where Cremer had set the note on the fender, and began to read aloud as though for the benefit of the others.

> Tell everyone we're sorry, but this is the only way. Jana, you would not agree to a divorce, and Merle and I will not go on without each other.
>
> Owen

Zerlow read it a second time, this time in silence.

"Well, that should explain the who and the why," he said to Cremer. With a half-wave at the Jeep, he continued, "and we certainly know the how and the where. Now, who gets to tell this Jana her husband has committed suicide along with his lover?"

Francis Cremer gave a long sigh. "I rather think that Jana might know more about this than we do," he said. "In any case we had better talk to her first, before we draw any conclusions about the how of this case. This was not a suicide."

▸ *What convinced Francis Cremer to look for something other than suicide as the cause of death?*

3

A Clever Solution at the County Fair

▼

It took only a couple of seconds for Chris Fogolin to realize that the change in his luck was holding. On the other side of the gently flapping canvas wall, the executive director of the Quail County Fair Board was shouting into the telephone. Chris could hear it as plainly as if J. Loudon Glint was talking to him directly.

"Who is this? Pincher? I thought so. Are you right there at the exhibit?" Glint was getting louder. The answer must have been affirmative for the next question was, "Well, can they hear you — Stipple and Two Feathers, I mean? Are they right there beside you, or . . . ?" There was the briefest of pauses and then a groan.

"Well, get private, for heaven sakes!" Glint was shouting now. "Why do you think we give you people cell phones! Honestly! . . . Yeah, yeah, yeah. Never mind that now! Look.

Check your watch. Call me back in exactly one minute. On the inside line."

There was a slight thump and then a loud honk as J. Loudon Glint cleared his nasal tracks before shouting once more. "Ellie! Bring me the entry forms on that homing pigeon exhibit! Right away!"

Ellie, who was also on the other side of the canvas wall, must have hesitated or looked perplexed because Glint came back immediately with, "Yes, all of them! There's only half a dozen entries in that class. I was down there this morning before the judging. Do I have to do everything myself?!"

Glint honked again. Twice. Chris was sympathetic. He too had a cold and wondered if that was what made the fair's executive director so cranky. Earlier that morning, Chris Fogolin had given serious thought to using his cold as an excuse to skip the county fair and stay in bed. His assignment was, all things considered, hardly the cutting edge of journalism. Chris was a crime reporter. Well, more accurately, that's what he wanted to be, but when one worked for the *Quail County Gleaner*, crime was limited to the police report on the second page, and most of that dealt with nothing more dramatic than stolen sheep. What would make the front page of *The Gleaner* tomorrow, and the day after, and the day after that, was news about the county fair. That more than anything else had gotten Chris out of bed. Better to have a by-line on the front page than no by-line at all.

Still, he'd spent the morning muttering under his breath about bad luck. Rain had begun to fall as soon as he entered the fair grounds. Bad for his cold and even worse for his shoes. Now there were not only cow patties to watch out for but mud too. And the rain had thinned the crowd, reducing the opportunity for a story. Even on *The Gleaner*, you had to have an angle to get on the front page.

But then the rain had brought good luck. A sudden

downpour had driven Chris into the swine and fowl tent — he'd been walking past it, having decided well in advance to pretend it wasn't even there — and the first person he spotted was Madonna Two Feathers. She was always good for news. Madonna Two Feathers was an advocate for Native American rights, and known well beyond the borders of Quail County for her less than discreet methods. If Madonna Two Feathers was here, Chris knew, there had to be a story somewhere. Even if it was only a picture of her with her beloved pigeons. That, in fact, was something he did immediately: photograph Madonna Two Feathers sitting in her wheelchair holding a pair of pigeons in a cage on her lap. He then took a close-up of the identifying tag on the cage. "Cream Rollers," it said, obviously referring to the breed. Underneath the tag, a blue rosette with a pair of trailing blue ribbons proclaimed "FIRST PRIZE."

Chris Fogolin had been working in Quail County long enough to be aware that this was not some simple pet-raising venture. Madonna Two Feathers and her family were internationally famous among pigeon fanciers. A prize-winning pair of Cream Rollers could fetch thousands from the right buyer.

That knowledge had made Chris hang around after the pictures were taken to peer at some of the other Cream Rollers. After all, the rain was still coming down. There were five other pairs of pigeons in the exhibit. To Chris, they all looked exactly the same, making him wonder how the judges went about making a decision. Despite himself, he had leaned closer to the line of metal cages, and it was then that he found his story. The exhibitor right beside Madonna Two Feathers was Maxwell Stipple. Stipple was almost as well known as his neighboring exhibitor, but not for the kind of news *The Gleaner* liked to print. Stipple was a self-proclaimed white supremacist who, only three weeks before, had paid a huge fine for distributing anti–Native American slogans in front of the courthouse.

For Chris, the opportunity was a golden one. Even *The Gleaner* would like his angle: pigeons as the great leveler, the reason to set aside ill will and racist ideas in the clean spirit of competition. He'd immediately finished a roll of film on the spot, and then, forgetting entirely about the rain, dashed off to find Madonna Two Feathers again. Stipple too, if he could. That had been an hour ago. In his excitement he'd almost forgotten his editor's principal instruction: to photograph and interview the 4-H Grand Champion. A feature for that was already half written for today's edition. With that obligation to see to, he'd lost track of both Stipple and Two Feathers, and as a last resort he had decided to turn to J. Loudon Glint, who, if he was certain to be part of the story, would be sure to help.

The sound of Glint's telephone brought Chris back to the present.

"Pincher? Yeah. OK. Yeah, yeah . . . Oh, no! Oh my God, what next?" Glint wasn't shouting anymore, but he could still be heard very easily. An office in a tent just didn't make for privacy.

"Well, who spoke to you first, Stipple or Two Feathers? Yeah, yeah. And Stipple says they're his Cream Rollers, and she says they're hers? Yeah, I know. They all look the same to me too. And he's claiming that the first-prize ribbon was for his birds and she switched the name tags? Or maybe the ribbons? Oh, great! I think — just a minute."

Glint stopped to put out a tremendous honk.

"Now, look. I can't leave here right now. Hey, there's no press there, is there? Good. Now here's what you do. Here's the solution. What you do is take the . . ."

"Sir!" It was Ellie, her large nose pushing right into Chris's face. "You can't be here, sir! This is a restricted area. It's for employees of the fair board only. Now if you need shelter from the rain, we're more than happy to . . ."

Chris didn't stick around for the rest of it. It would take at least five minutes to get across the fair grounds to the exhibit where Pincher was about to follow Glint's instructions, and Chris wanted to get some shots of it.

▶ *Chris knows what Glint told Pincher to do, even though Ellie interrupted at the time, and he's going to photograph it for his paper. What has Glint told Pincher to do?*

4

A Holdup at the Adjala Building

▼

It was only 4:00 PM on a clear midsummer day, but Jeff Ercul expected the street to be in shadows by now. That was yet another reason he had come to deeply regret the transfer from Loretto to the city: urban canyons — long, winding tubes of semi-darkness between rows of skyscrapers.

On this particular stretch of Richmond Street, however, the buildings on the other side were quite a bit shorter than the norm, a tribute to the days when an environmentally sensitive city council had put height restriction bylaws into effect. For that reason, the sun was still lighting up the south and west sides of the Adjala Building, its unique coppery sides and floating design making the kind of grand and lofty statement that prompted even bored frequent fliers to lean over from their aisle seats to get a look.

Jeff squinted as he stood in front of the Adjala Building's

main doors. Unlike the outside walls of the building, which were paneled with metal, these were thick plate glass, although they had the same copper tint. It was a glorious building, no question. There was nothing like it in Loretto, where he had spent his first five years on the force. Loretto didn't have live theater either, or big league sports, or the incredible restaurants, or the astounding variety of shopping opportunities. But then, it didn't have crack either, or doors with multiple locks, or people with "subway-elbows," or slums, or beggars on the streets.

The transfer to the city had been offered to Jeff as an avenue to promotion.

"You want to make sergeant," the Human Resources weenie had pointed out to him. You can't sit up there in the boonies for another five years. You gotta get some time where the action is."

Actually, the decision had been easy; Jeff wanted to make sergeant. And the truth was, he really had believed the city would make him feel more like a cop. But the feeling didn't last long. It wasn't just the amount of crime here, and the nature of it. And it wasn't just his disappointment at Twelfth Precinct headquarters. (At first glance, and ever afterwards, it looked to Jeff like a Third World bus station.) Nor was it things like the downtown streets blocking out the sun. He wanted to go back home because, somehow, crime was different there. Not just that there was less of it, and indeed there was much less. Rather, it was more the fact that crime was harder to commit. People watched out for other people. They knew what was going on, and they cared. Here, nobody watched. It was an urban virtue to be isolated from what was going on around you.

Take the theft he was investigating right now, a holdup in broad daylight, just before lunch, right here where he was standing. Not a single witness could be found. Even the victim had not seen the thief.

A courier carrying bearer bonds had felt a gun in her back — an iffy point in Jeff's view; she said it was a gun, but she hadn't seen it, only felt it. The thief had ordered her to stand still and not turn around. Then he'd pulled the strap off her shoulder and over her head, taking her delivery bag.

"Then he says . . . he says . . ." This had all been reported to Jeff through an enormous wad of bubble gum. "He says, 'Walk inside the building. Look straight ahead. You turn around, you're finished.' So, like, what'm I gonna do? Like, I mean, I'm not gonna take a chance. But I'm gonna play it smart, see? Like, I'm in this building all the time. An' I know there's this security guard by the elevators. So I go in like the guy says, an' I don't turn around. An' then I run for the guard."

At this point the gum began to pop with even greater ferocity.

"An', well, like you know the rest. Jerk's not there! Whatsa point of havin' security? Right?

"Anyways. That's all I know. 'Cept fer his voice. The holdup guy. Told you that b'fore. It's, like, really deep, the voice. Like that actor. You know, whaddayacallim . . . James Earl Jones. That guy."

Jeff sighed deeply. He found he was doing a lot of that lately. Sighing. This would not have happened in Loretto, he was sure. He sighed again, wondering whether, by putting pressure on the courier, maybe arresting her, or threatening her, he could get her to tell the truth.

▸ *Jeff Ercul has determined that there is a flaw in the account the courier has given him. What is that flaw?*

5

A Surprise Witness for the Highland Press Case

▼

Normally, Jane Forrester didn't waste her time even thinking about buying a lottery ticket. The logic of such a move, given the odds of winning, had always eluded her.

It was only after she left The Toby Jug, the day before Christmas, that Jane gave the idea serious consideration for the very first time. Standing there in the parking lot, digging in her purse for her car keys, it occurred to her that she might well be on a streak of good luck.

First, there was the matter of bumping into Wally Birks. Well, not just bumping; she'd walked right into him. Almost knocked him over. She'd been heading for the one empty stool at the bar in The Toby Jug, then suddenly changed her mind and walked to the back to use the washroom. With her thoughts on trying to identify just which one of the patrons was Wally Birks, she crashed into the back of a man in a blue parka who'd stopped suddenly at the entrance to the little alcove. Directly ahead a bright red door said "Private." On the left wall was the "Ladies" door, and opposite it the "Gents." Both in bright red.

Funny how she remembered the colors: the red doors and his blue parka, and the truly ugly carpeting. Ocher. Who on earth picks ocher?

Probably the colors stuck because of the phone call just before noon.

"You're Forrester, they tell me, Jane Forrester?" a gravelly and very pedantic voice had asked. "Well, I'm Birks, Wally Birks. That's Walter of course, but the only one ever called me Walter was my mother, and actually, she's been dead now, oh, some twenty years. Even my teachers never called me Walter —"

"Sir!" Jane broke in before she got a life history complete with favorite foods. "You wanted to speak to me about something, sir?"

"Well, actually . . . yes. You see, I've been sitting here thinking. Got lots of time to do that now. Actually, I'm retired, you see, and —"

"Sir! Could you tell me what it is you wanted to speak about?" Jane was trying to keep the edge out of her voice.

"OK. Yes. Right. Sure. The Highland Press thing. Outside The Toby Jug? That's my favorite pub. And I saw something . . . Well, actually, I should have called you before this, but you see, a person doesn't always want to get involved, now, does he? And I was thinking . . . Matter of fact, I was just saying to my brother-in-law the other day . . ."

Despite herself, Jane held off interrupting. The Highland Press case was one of the open files on her desk, and every lead had been exhausted. Only a plum like a surprise witness was going to give her a break.

"... so I was thinking, actually, I should meet you there. At the pub?"

Jane took a deep breath. "Yes, sir. That sounds like a good idea. Could we meet this afternoon?"

"Actually, I was just going to suggest that. I'll be there wearing a grey parka so you'll know who I am. It's got a nice black fur trim on the hood. My daughter and son-in-law gave it to me for Christmas two years ago. They live —"

"Mr. Birks, can you be there at three o'clock?"

"Well, now, I suppose I could. You see, the pub's right on the way to —"

"That's great, Mr. Birks. See you then. Bye for now."

Between the time of that call and her visit to The Toby Jug, Jane Forrester tried without success to put Wally Birks out of her mind. It was obvious he was the kind of person who could make the Charge of the Light Brigade sound like instructions for repotting azaleas, but the Highland Press case was a stickler, and if he could help, then . . .

As it turned out, Jane's time at the pub was mercifully brief. When she apologized to the man in the blue parka, he turned around very slowly.

"Now, I recognize that voice, don't I, Jane Forrester? Actually, I was wondering how we'd meet. This is a pretty big place. And busy. I have to go in there, you see." With his thumb he pointed over his shoulder at the doors. "At my age, a person has to, well, I don't want to talk about that to a lady. But you see, the thing is, I don't have my grey parka on like I told you I would. You'd never guess what happened. I went out to the back porch to get it. You see, before my wife got sick we had the porch closed in. She always called it 'the sun room' after that. I could never get used to that. A porch is a porch, I always say."

At that very moment, another piece of good luck happened. Jane's beeper screamed at her, and even before she'd scanned for the number, she was saying, "Oh, Mr. Birks. I'm so dreadfully sorry. An emergency. Look, I have to go. Now, someone from my office will call you for your information. It won't be me. One of my colleagues."

With that, she'd spun on her heels and disappeared before Wally Birks could wind up again.

Three bits of luck, she thought to herself in the parking lot, each saving her from wasting time with Wally Birks on the Highland Press case. Definitely worth considering a lottery ticket.

▸ *Jane Forrester's accidental bump, and her beeper sounding, are two bits of good luck. The third is the clue that tells her Wally is likely not a reliable informant, for he's already lied to her once. What is that lie?*

6

THE CASE OF THE MISSING .38 SMITH AND WESSON

▼

G ary Westlake made a mental note to find out who had been the last to use Number 9119. The car had come to life when he turned on the ignition, and he hated that. One by one he turned off the radio, the windshield wipers, the fan, the rear defrost, while he waited for the engine to warm. Whoever it was, he noted with even more annoyance, had even left the glove compartment door hanging open. All this, along with an accumulation of junk on the passenger seat: gum wrappers, a ratty toque (certainly not a regulation item but sometimes the highway patrol used them), a flashlight that should have been returned to its holder under the dash and what appeared to be a forgotten, half-completed accident report.

With one hand, Gary scooped up the mess and tossed it into the back seat. "There's one slob in this department," he said out loud, "who's going to be very sorry the Chief had to use a patrol car today!"

Gary had a fully developed passion for order and neatness. He began to plan, even enjoy, the substance of the anticipated chewout as he clamped the transmitter switch twice.

"Go ahead." Central Dispatch, at least, was doing exactly what it was supposed to do.

"Westlake here. I'm exiting the lot right now. Expect to return by 3:00 PM If there's . . ."

"Chief! We were just going to all-call you. Lowinski wants you. Says it's urgent."

Gary toyed for a moment with ignoring the request. New people on patrol had a way of failing to separate true urgency from simple impatience. Besides, he had a throbbing toothache. "Patch her through," he replied tiredly. He knew he couldn't entertain the thought of ignoring a call from a rookie.

Almost instantly the young policewoman was in contact. "Sir? Chief Westlake?" Gary hated Lowinski's habit of speaking in the interrogative. It made her sound like a teenager, which, come to think of it, he realized, she almost was! She was only twenty-one. "This is Chief Westlake." He tried not to sound gruff, but his tooth really hurt.

"Ah! Chief? The Packers case? I think I have something? You know the gun? The missing gun? A .38 Smith and Wesson, right? I'm holding a guy here. You better . . . uh . . . do you want to see for yourself?"

The Packers case was an unsolved murder, the first murder, solved or unsolved, in the seven years since Gary had become chief. One of the missing links was the murder weapon. Ballistic information had told them what it was, but that was as far as anyone on the case had been able to get.

"Slow down, Lowinski," Gary said, as much to himself as to the young woman on patrol. He could feel excitement in spite of himself, in spite of his aching tooth and the mess in 9119. "First of all, where are you?"

Lowinski was not about to slow down. "On King Road? East? I'm at . . . at . . ." The voice grew faint, then loud again. "At . . . in front of 414, okay? 414 King Road."

"All right. Hang on." Gary took a deep breath and thought for a moment. A .38 Smith and Wesson was hardly something out of the ordinary. If it was only an unlicensed gun, then he'd be smarter to let Lowinski handle it herself. Good experience. But then . . .

"Lowinski. Are you all right? Do you need help?"

"No, sir, I'm fine. I have the susp — I mean, I have a possible arrest in the car. There's no trouble, okay? You want I should bring him in?"

"No. Yes! I mean . . . wait a minute, Lowinski."

Gary's toothache, which had been coming and going in waves, was gathering strength for another surge. He waited, but it didn't come.

"Uh . . . Lowinski? The Smith and Wesson? What's fishy about it?" Gary wondered if he, too, wasn't beginning to speak in the interrogative.

"No license."

Gary almost groaned.

"I stop him a few minutes ago, right? Tail light out. And I think I smell booze, right?"

Against his better judgment Gary answered, "Right."

"So. Routine check. I open the trunk. And there it is in the trunk. The gun?"

It occurred to Gary that Lowinski was not only interrogative in her style, she also spoke entirely in the present tense. What makes you think it has anything to do with the Packers case?" he asked.

"Smith and Wesson, right?"

"Lowinski, we've been through that." The wave of ache

had only been teasing before. Now it had arrived in force.

"Yeah, but that's it! The guy says he just found it! Like, this morning?"

Were it anything but the Packers case, Gary would have made a second mental note: to have Lowinski take speech therapy. Instead he responded, "*Found* it? Where?"

"You know the construction on King Road? At the edge of town? On the east? Toward Nobleton? Just at the bottom of the hill?"

"Lowinski, I know where it is!" One more question on top of the toothache would have tipped him over the edge.

"Well, the guy says he saw it lying in one of the big puddles there, right? Says he figures somebody ditched it. So he picks it up? Says he hasn't had time to turn it in. Okay?"

Gary heard himself say, "And you've, like, got him in your car now, right?" Whatever Lowinski's response, he didn't hear it. He was staring in shock at himself in the rear-view mirror. "Lowinski, you've done well," he finally said. "Sit tight. I'll be there in two minutes."

He pulled the shift lever down into Drive, but before accelerating wiped a smudged fingerprint off the speedometer glass with a gloved hand. More dirt, he thought. "Lowinski! You still there?"

"Yes, Chief?"

"Lowinski, what car did you have yesterday?"

"Number 8228. The same one I always have. Why?"

"Never mind."

► *Apparently, Gary Westlake agrees with Lowinski that she has a possible suspect in the Packers case, and it's because of the gun. Why?*

7

A 9-1-1 CALL FROM WHITBY TOWERS

▼

Bev Ashby was so distracted by the size of the crowd gathered on the sidewalk that at first she didn't hear the concierge shouting at her.

"They're up there!" He was bent over the driver's door, yelling red-faced at the closed window and gesticulating wildly at the building across the sidewalk. "Fourth floor! But you have to walk 'cause the elevator's been down since yesterday!"

It wasn't until several hours later that Bev ruefully acknowledged, yet again, that maybe it's true what they say about cops: they just stick out. For the life of her she had no idea how the concierge had identified her, first as a police officer, and second, as the detective sent to investigate the incident. She was dressed in civvies, the car was unmarked, and she had used neither siren nor light. And there were several other cars at the curb that were clearly sent there by a police dispatcher. Yet the concierge had run out the revolving doors of Whitby Towers directly to her.

"Your uniformed people are up there! Two of them!" Bev had her window rolled down, but now he was yelling even louder. "And the chauffeur that saw him do it!"

His shouting increased the size of the crowd and drew their attention away from the incident that was entertaining them in the middle of the busy downtown street. A noontime fender bender had developed into a slugfest between the two drivers involved. Both were now draped over the hoods of their respective cars in handcuffs.

Bev had to push the concierge back to get out of the car. He was still waving his arms and sputtering.

"I'm the one that called 9-1-1," he said into her face. "The chauffeur saw him doing it from down here on the street! Hanging himself! Yelled at me to call and then ran for the stairs!" The young man wasn't shouting anymore, but he was still wound up enough to draw even more of the crowd toward them. Bev took him by the arm and forced her way through the gawkers toward the doors of Whitby Towers.

"Shouldn't this be *your* job?" she said over her shoulder. "I mean, you're the one supposed to be breaking trail, aren't you?"

"Yes, Omigod! Look, I'm sorry! This is only my second day. And I . . . like . . . I've never called 9-1-1 before! And I . . ."

Bev pushed through to the revolving doors with the concierge in tow. Once inside, the plush quietness of the lobby calmed him with dramatic suddenness.

"Fourth floor," the concierge said with professional detachment. "Number 411. The stairs are over there behind that pillar. We're very sorry about the elevator problem."

Bev nodded. "I'll be back down in a while to talk to you. Just don't leave, please."

By the time she reached the fourth floor she was puffing a bit. She wondered how the occupants of Whitby Towers were tolerating a two-day elevator failure. It was an expensive building and even though "Towers" was an enormously pretentious title — the place had only six floors — a lot of money was needed for the rent here.

Suite 411 was easy enough to find, for a uniformed officer was standing in the hallway outside the door. He tipped his cap with his index finger as Bev approached. "Body's inside, Lieutenant. We have not cut him down; we've only been here," he looked at his watch, "seventeen minutes now. Chauffeur's in there with my partner."

He held the door open for Bev so she could see the entire tableau before taking a step. Suite 411 was a luxuriously appointed studio apartment. What marred the sight of the deep pile rug and highly polished reproduction furniture was the body of a silver-haired man, in excellent trim, hanging from a thin nylon rope, an overturned chair at his lifeless feet.

"His name is . . ." The patrolman started to speak, but Bev cut him off with a shake of her head. Twice she walked slowly around the body and then expanded the circle to walk around the room. Everything was in perfect order as one would expect at Whitby Towers. Well, not quite everything. The telephone wire was cut. Actually, not cut. Torn. That had taken strength. There was something else, too. Bev bent over in front of the balcony doors. What was it on the floor there, one end of a shoelace? No. Nylon rope. Looked like the same stuff that was around the dead man's neck. With a pen, she spread the drapes just enough to follow the rope to about knee level where the other end was clamped between the doors.

Nodding to herself, Bev looked up at the uniformed officer. "Now you can tell me his name," she said to him.

"On second thought," she turned to the chauffeur, "you go first. Let's start with your name."

"Sandford Verity." No hesitation. He responded as though he'd anticipated her question. And he didn't talk the way Bev thought a chauffeur might, but then, she had to admit, she didn't really know any chauffeurs. Maybe they all talk this way! "What happened is very simple." He continued as though he were in charge. "My firm is Brock Livery Service. We pick up Mr. Seneca every day — that's his name: Audley Seneca — at 11:50 and take him to wherever he directs. It's a standing, daily order. Yesterday and today I came up here to his suite, because of the elevator situation, instead of meeting him in the lobby. You see, he has a prosthesis, an artificial leg actually, and the stairs are somewhat of a problem for him. This morning when I arrived I happened to look up. Thought maybe he might be watching that altercation on the street. That's when I saw him on the chair there, the rope around his neck. Of course I ran as fast as I could. Told the concierge to call 9-1-1. But I got here too late. The door was locked. What I should have done, I realize now, was get the concierge to come with me. With a master key. But then, after a crisis is over, one always thinks of things one should have done."

"Agreed, Mr. Verity," Bev said and turned to the uniformed officer. "Would you go down to the lobby," she said, "and bring the concierge up here? There's quite a big hole here in the story of Mr. Seneca's alleged suicide."

► *What is the "big hole" to which Bev Ashby refers?*

8

BEFORE THE FIRST
COMMERCIAL BREAK

▼

Director's Note: Edit this section to three minutes ten seconds. Insert between credit and first commercial break.

SCENE ONE

Camera Notes for Storyboard, Scene One:
#1. Pull back so that entire prison building can be seen. Gilhooley appears from inside prison in distance and walks into camera toward gate. Hold until Gilhooley reaches gate. #2. Track him to motorcycle west of gate where rider is already astride. Move in as Gilhooley boards motorcycle behind rider. Hold close for a view of back and side of rider. Pick up rider's leather vest, cutoff T-shirt, long hair, and

snake tattoo down length of left arm.
#3. Track left to follow motorcycle as it drives away and out of shot.
#4. Fade to black.

FX, Scene One:
Sound of Gilhooley's footsteps builds as he walks toward camera. Voiceover of Assistant Warden Brackish starts after footsteps are established. Sound of idling motorcycle comes in over Brackish's last words. Motorcycle sound follows Gilhooley and rider out of scene and fades.

Script, Scene One:
ASSISTANT WARDEN LEONARD BRACKISH: (in voiceover) Getting to be a habit, Mr. Gilhooley, isn't it? What's this, our third goodbye? No. Let's call it an *au revoir*. Men like you, Gilhooley . . . it's not a case of if but when. You'll be back, and I'll be waiting. You're bad, Gilhooley. Just bad seed. Like a snake. You can't help yourself. You're poison.

SCENE TWO

Camera Notes for Storyboard, Scene Two:
#1. Establishing shot of seedy storefront from across street.
#2. Move in and pan slowly left to right over gold lettering on door: RARE COINS AND ESTATE JEWELRY
#3. Continue panning right, pulling back until shot encompasses Gilhooley talking to another man on sidewalk. Arms are moving to emphasize what he is saying. Man has snake tattoo on arm. Might be biker from Scene One but dressed better. Listens and nods. No face.
#4. Continue pan past two men and fade to black.

FX, Scene Two:
City traffic noises.

No Voices in Scene Two

SCENE THREE

Camera Notes for Storyboard, Scene Three:
#1. Inside store at rear. Full shot. Gilhooley stands on one side of rear door and police officer on other side. Gilhooley wears slacks and shirt with long sleeves rolled to just above wrist. He is cowering. Officer is in uniform. Her stance is confrontational. One hand on door handle as though to keep Gilhooley from running. On the floor between them is a revolver. Back of butt is against the door so that muzzle points at camera. To the officer's left and in front, Katzmann sits in a wooden chair.
#2. When Katzmann begins talking, move back to pick up array of shelves above him and scatter of diamond and ruby rings on working surface behind him. Katzmann wears loupe like a monocle, raised to his forehead. All his dialogue is emphasized by a rigidly pointed index finger at Gilhooley, the officer, and the door.
#3. Gilhooley gives impression he'd like to be sucked into the wall. Throughout scene fingers the barrel of the middle hinge on the door. While talking, retreats back along the wall a few inches but continues to hold the hinge as if for security. With right hand gropes behind him feeling for a small table just inches away, but never makes contact until the final shot.
#4. Gilhooley's hand bumps the small table, nearly upsetting a cup of coffee in a Styrofoam cup. He turns to rescue it and for a split second reveals a snake tattoo on his arm.
#5. Fade to black.

No FX in Scene Three

Script, Scene Three:
KATZMANN: . . . and two minutes after I see Gilhooley talking to this guy — another bum — the guy's in here with his gun out. He's been tipped off, no question. 'Cause he comes right to the back here. This is where all the good stuff is, the really valuable pieces. I mean, how does the guy know to do that unless he's been told? Right, Gilhooley?

GILHOOLEY: I didn't say nothin' t' him 'bout that.

KATZMANN: And there's no way the guy's going to know I've got the safe open this morning to work on the new stuff unless he's been told. And, AND, who leaves the security screen wide open? The one separating this area from the rest of my store? You see what I get, officer, for hiring parolees? If it wasn't for my alarm system . . . I dunno. As it was, I thought he was going to shoot me anyway. When the alarm went off, I mean. But he panicked. Dropped his gun and run out the back door. That's when his partner here came back.

GILHOOLEY: Look, it just ain't like that! He — like, Katzmann — sends me across the street for coffee. That's every morning this time. The guy on the street? I never seen him before. He was just askin' directions. Alls I know is I come back here with the coffee and the alarm's ringin' and then you cops come in. I don't know nothin' what he's talkin' about!

► *If it is the director's intent to have viewers wonder whether Gilhooley is guilty or is being set up, then the director is going to have to correct a serious mistake before these scenes are shot. What is that mistake?*

9

To Catch a Mannerly Thief

▼

A s she stepped over the potholes in the street and leaned
hard into a fierce east wind, Agnes Skeehan made a
promise to herself: never again was she going to attend a conference in November unless it was within walking distance of
the equator. Actually, for Agnes, anywhere warmer than
Liverpool would do. Liverpool may have produced the
Beatles, and it could point with pride at its importance to the
Industrial Revolution, but to Agnes that was hardly enough
to make up for the miserable weather.

She mounted the curb, trotted across the sidewalk, and
pulled hard at the entrance door of her hotel. Three days at
the Birkenhead Arms had taught Agnes to yank with both
hands at the ancient portal.

"Ah, young missy!" It was the hotel porter. He made a

contribution all his own to Agnes's opinion of Liverpool. "You've got a telephone message here, young missy. All the way from Canada! A Deputy Commissioner Mowat. Sounds important, missy. Talked to him myself, I did. Told him you were out, I did."

Agnes mumbled a thank you as she grabbed the message and ran for the creaky old elevator. As things stood at the moment, she was only three hours away from her flight home, but she had a feeling this call was going to change her schedule.

It did.

"I want you to stay over there in Liverpool and help them with this case." Deputy Commissioner Mowat's voice crackled and sputtered across the Atlantic only minutes later. "As a favor from us, you know, international police cooperation and all that." He paused, but then jumped in again as though to head off the objection he was expecting. "You're simply the best there is on handwriting. They don't have anybody that comes close to you. Now what I want you to do right away is go to their headquarters — it's right by your hotel there — and report to Superintendent Anthony Opilis. He's the head of their CID: their Criminal Investigation Department. Now what I want you to do is consider yourself on temporary assignment there. Indefinite. As long as it takes."

Agnes struggled so hard to keep from telling Deputy Commissioner Mowat where he could stuff the international cooperation and the temporary assignment that she barely heard the rest. She didn't really need to though. The tabloids were full of the case that prompted his call. "The Friendly Filcher" one daily called it. "The Case of the Courteous Cat Burglar" another dubbed it. Whatever he — or she — deserved to be called, the case involved an amazingly successful thief who was breaking into homes and stealing jewelry. He seemed to have a peculiar respect for his victims, and this, in addition to the size of the take, was what the papers found so interesting. At each theft — there had been seven now — the thief left behind a neatly handwritten note of apology and an assurance that the stolen pieces would find their way only into the hands of people who would appreciate their beauty and value.

These notes, Agnes knew, were the reason she was being loaned to the Liverpool CID. Mowat was right when he called her the best. Agnes Skeehan, *Corporal* Agnes Skeehan, fourteen-year veteran of the Royal Canadian Mounted Police, had a special interest and an even more special knack in handwriting analysis. At graduation from the police training college in Regina, circumstances had presented her with a choice of more study, or assignment to a mounted patrol at the Parliament Buildings in Ottawa. Since race-track betting windows were as close to horses as Agnes ever cared to be, she picked the study and had never looked back. Eight months ago, her article in the Journal of Forensic Science had led to an invitation to address a conference in Liverpool. Little did she realize when she came down from the podium there, to a huge round of applause, that the next move would be, not to the airport, but into the superintendent's office at the Liverpool CID.

Superintendent Opilis, a long-time acquaintance of Deputy Commissioner Mowat as it turned out, was a plodder. His explanation of the jewelry thefts to Agnes was so detailed and so slow that she had to fight to pay attention. She kept turning her head toward the grimy office window to yawn, covering the move with a phoney cough.

The superintendent must have sensed her mood for suddenly Agnes became aware of annoyance in his voice.

"Withenshawe?" he said, or rather, asked. "I say, Corporal

Skeehan. You heard me? Withenshawe Purveyors?"

Agnes blushed. She had indeed been drifting. The problem was, she just didn't want to be in Liverpool.

"Yes, Superintendent, I'm sorry." She got up and walked to the window, trying to appear alert by focusing on a weathervane pointing at her from atop a pub across the street.

"Withenshawe Purveyors of Speke Street." She cleared her throat. "Every one of the notes was written on Withenshawe's letterhead. I'm aware of that. And your people have definitely established that they were all written by the same left-handed person. I'm aware of that, too. But don't you think the Withenshawe Purveyors stationery is a most clumsy red herring? After all, who . . ."

"Indeed, indeed Corporal Skeehan." Opilis got up and joined Agnes at the window. "But you see, there are other serious reasons why Alistair Withenshawe is a right handy suspect." He paused awkwardly. "We . . . er . . . we've summoned him. His office is just a short walk south of here. What we want you to do is . . . Why! That's him! Right there. Across the street."

"Him?" Agnes pointed at a tall, very nattily dressed gentleman holding down a bowler hat. "The dude with the hat? And the cane? Look at him!" Agnes was fully awake now. "Does he always walk like that in public?"

"Yes, well," Superintendent Opilis was almost apologetic. "Ah, we have dealt with him before. I'm afraid he's a bit of a showman."

To prove the policeman's point, Alistair Withenshawe, who had been bouncing his cane off the edge of the curb and catching it, now began to twirl it high in the air like a drum major, spinning it first over one parked car, then the next, and then a third, before he brought it down and made a crisp military turn off the walk and into the street toward the police station.

Opilis let a touch of admiration creep into his voice. "Snappy, what?"

Agnes looked at him. "Yes, I agree. Snappy. But I'll give you any odds you want he didn't write those notes."

► *Why is Agnes Skeehan so sure of that?*

10

SOMETHING SUSPICIOUS
IN THE HARBOR

▼

Sue Meisner brough both oars forward into the little row-boat and drifted until the boat bumped against the huge freighter. It was especially dark down here on the water between the two big ocean-going ships. She felt as though she were in a tunnel, with the superstructure of the *Christopher Thomas* looming over her and the even bigger Russian ship alongside, completing the arch. Still there was enough light from the city to see the mark from early this morning, the little paint scrape where Sue had bumped against the *Christopher Thomas* the first time.

That had been with the police boat though, and Sue had been acting officially, as a constable with the Metropolitan Toronto Police marine unit. However, there was nothing offi-cial about this trip. It was anything but. She was in restricted waters to boot. Tiny, privately operated rowboats were not welcome in the main channel of Toronto harbor, and Sue knew if she were caught there, it would be hard to imagine what would be worse: her embarrassment or Inspector Braemore's wrath.

That was why, at sunset, she had taken the ferry from the city over to Ward's Island, collected the rowboat, and then pulled her way across the channel in the dark. By staying close to the piers along Cherry Street, she'd reached the *Christopher Thomas* undetected. So far anyway.

Sue shifted on the seat to relieve her sore back. The movement caused the little craft to rock, and it banged hard into the side of the freighter. The rowboat was aluminum, and to her, the sound in the tunnel between the two larger vessels was like a gunshot. But she knew it wouldn't be heard on deck. With the racket up there and in the hold, especially from the noisy diesels powering the loading winches, there wasn't a chance even for normal conversation, let alone picking up a sound from the surface of the water.

The crew of the *Christopher Thomas* had been loading big containers full of automobile engines for several hours already when Sue and her partner had made their official visit that morning. The two officers were responding to a tip. Sue had taken the call herself right after coming on duty.

"Something crooked in the harbor," the caller had said. "On the *Christopher Thomas* and maybe that Russian one beside her — the *Potemkin* something. You people should go check." Then the caller had hung up.

Inspector Braemore had not been very impressed. It was his opinion that some disgruntled sailor wanted to harass the shipowners and was using the police to do it. And Sue's visit this morning, if anything, seemed to confirm that, for they'd seen nothing amiss. She and her partner had circled the ship inside and outside. There were no safety violations, no evidence of contraband, not even a suggestion of drug use in the crew's quarters. The *Christopher Thomas* appeared to be just a freighter being filled with cargo by a busy crew that did not want two police officers getting in their way.

It was Inspector Braemore's I-told-you-so expression that had got Sue's dander up. It explained why, later in her shift, she had stood on the nearby ferry docks for half an hour and watched the loading through binoculars, and why she'd checked the ship's papers twice with the harbormaster. And it also explained — or so she told herself — why sore back and all, she was sitting in a tiny rowboat in the smelly darkness of Toronto harbor long after sunset.

"Well," she said out loud, "at least, it's paid off. At least now I *know* there is certainly something crooked going on. Tomorrow morning there's going to be another inspection so we can find out just what it is!"

► *What has led Sue Meisner to the conclusion that something crooked is going on aboard the* Christopher Thomas?

11

Esty Wills Prepares for a Business Trip

▼

The elevator was agonizingly slow. It was overheated too, and smelly, filled with the odor of institutional cleanser, and cooking smells that provided an unwelcome and unasked-for accounting of who had what for dinner the previous night. Still, it gave Sean Hennigar a twinge of mildly vindictive pleasure. All things being equal, the apartment was a dump, a major comedown in lifestyle for Esty Wills — Mr. Flash, as he was called in the D.A.'s office.

Sean moved to lean against the back wall but then thought better of it. No point in having the graffiti come off on his overcoat. Certainly he wanted no souvenir of a visit to Esty Wills, even if the visit was part of his job. Sean was a parole officer, working out of the D.A.'s office in Market Square. Esty Wills was one of his "files." His least favorite: Wills was a notorious con man, well known in Chicago. Nightclubs knew him as a big spender. Mercedes-Benz and Lexus dealerships vied for his attention. Chi-Vegas Charters automatically bumped passengers to suit his demands, and everyone working for the Blackhawks, Cubs, or Bulls knew his seating preferences.

On the other side of the coin, insurance companies had tagged his name on all their software programs. So had practically every police department in northern Illinois. And although the Consumer Protection Agency had not used Wills's name in a recent flyer to seniors, it was clearly him the group had in mind. To Sean Hennigar, and everyone else in the D.A.'s office for that matter, Esty Wills was nothing but an unrepentant career crook who consumed an entirely disproportionate amount of their time and who, despite his convictions, still seemed to be able to wheedle privileges out of the department.

Take now, for example. Wills was about to leave Chicago for three days on a business trip to Asunción, a clear violation of the conditions of his parole. He had served only four months of his three-year sentence before being paroled (to no one's surprise) and was already applying for special exemptions. In a classic Wills deal, he had managed to have himself retained by the International Monetary Fund, a partner with the Japanese government in an experimental project investigating the viability of growing mulberry bushes in Paraguay, the ultimate object being the raising of silkworms.

The Banco Nacional de Fomento had leaned on the Japanese representatives, who had leaned on the IMF, who had leaned on an assistant deputy secretary at Commerce in Washington, who had leaned on the Cook County D.A., who promptly signed the permission-to-travel form and then called Sean into his office. Wheels spinning wheels, and now Sean was bringing the form to Wills.

Sean reached out to knock on the door of 14B. He couldn't

help noting that somehow Wills had snagged a corner apartment. The door opened immediately to reveal a loudly dressed middle-aged man in standard used-car salesman pose. He was holding a wool sock in one hand.

"Don't they come in pairs?" Sean asked without any preliminary. It took Wills aback, but only for a second.

"Ah!" He smiled beneficently. "My favorite mother hen is becoming a wit! What next? A song and dance?"

Sean stepped into the apartment without waiting for an invitation. He wasn't smiling. Nor did he take the bait. "Let's get this over with," he said. "Show me your ticket and visa, and I'll give you your passport."

Reading Sean's mood, Wills led the way across the small bachelor suite to where his suitcase sat open on a chesterfield, and extracted the two items requested. Sean looked at the airline ticket very closely. At first, he hardly noticed the discrepancy, distracted as he was by the scarf and gloves labeled L. L. Bean and by the other wool sock. Esty Wills was buying from mail order catalogues, it seemed. A far cry from the personal tailor he'd been used to. This gave Sean an inordinate amount of satisfaction, but only briefly, until the ticket upset him.

"Four days?" He frowned at Wills. "What are you trying to pull here!"

Wills spread his hands in another used-car salesman gesture. "Gimme a break! It's travel time! I got to go via Buenos Aires, and connect there to go back north to Asunción. Takes almost a day. Same thing coming back. And I need two days there. Look, phone the IMF if you want. Or Washington!"

Sean tossed the ticket at the suitcase, and then very reluctantly followed it with Wills's passport. Without another word, he left the apartment and walked down the hall to where the slow elevator waited for him. All the way down he felt uneasy, bothered by something he couldn't put his finger on. The uneasiness stayed with him through the tiny lobby into the parking lot, where he took a minute to blow a skiff of snow off the windshield and peer into Esty Wills's car.

The used stub of a bus ticket on the front seat said Chicago–St. Louis Return. The thought of Esty Wills traveling by bus should have given Sean some satisfaction. The fact too that the car was a two-year-old Pontiac should have reinforced the feeling. But it didn't. Somehow, Sean couldn't shake the conviction that Esty Wills was not going to Asunción, but for the life of him, Sean couldn't figure out what had triggered that thought.

The suspicion bothered him even more as he left the parking lot. It wasn't helped, either, when he noticed that the Pontiac was in the choicest parking spot in the lot. "Reserved: 14B" had been painted recently on the little sign on the curb.

► *What is nagging at Sean Hennigar? Other than the fact that Esty Wills is a known con man, which would make one suspect him in any case, what is it that has twigged Sean's subconscious?*

12

THE POWER
OF CHANCE

▼

After thirty-seven years on the bench, Tom Houghton had
developed a pretty dim view of the role of chance in
human affairs. He was by nature a logical person, and tended
to view the world that way. Chance, in his opinion, was an
explanatory last resort for those who didn't have the brains
or the will to think things through. But after what had
happened yesterday afternoon, he knew he just might have to
revise that point of view.

The chain of events — chances — began in his court late
yesterday morning in a break-and-enter case: two teenage
boys and a girl, all three well past the young offender stage.
The third prosecution witness had just raised his right hand,
and the "I swear" had come out with a bellow. Tom wasn't
sure whether the man was being defiant or just loud.

Whichever it was, with only those two words, he'd made everyone in the court look up sharply.

The witness was a big man, maybe fifty, fifty-five, Tom thought, with a huge distended beer belly. His belt was slung so low it looked more like a truss than something to hold up his pants. The belly and the loud "I swear" triggered recall of a paragraph in the pretrial report. This must be Walter Hope, Tom realized, the one they called Whispering Hope — no wonder! He was the construction worker who claimed to have overheard the kids trying to deal goods on the patio of the Lagoon Saloon.

Tom tried to catch the eye of the young prosecuting attorney before she got started. Not only was she young, she was new, and this could turn into a lengthy examination. Sometime later, Tom was to acknowledge to himself that it was at this very point that "chance" might have taken over.

A double shot of chance, actually. The first unusual occurrence was that the Yankees played the Blue Jays that afternoon, one of those rare midweek 1:30 starts. The second was that Tom had tickets, and it really wasn't his turn for them. He and four others had a pair of seasons. They called themselves the Twenty Percent Club, for at the beginning of the schedule each year they divided the tickets five ways. Tom's Yankee game for this series would normally have been the next night, but weeks ago he'd made a trade. Chance?

Whatever the chain of circumstance, there was no way he was going to miss the first pitch no matter how slowly the wheels of justice might grind as a result, and so, very unobtrusively, he gave the high sign to Maurice Marchand standing at the back.

"Just a minute, Ms. Dankert." Tom caught the prosecutor before she stood up.

Maurice, the bailiff, saw the signal and walked urgently to the bench. Just as urgently, he whispered in Tom's ear, making very definitive movements with both hands. It was an old ploy that Tom Houghton rarely used, but, well, a Yankees game was a Yankees game.

"I'm afraid it will be necessary to adjourn," Tom announced to the court.

Maurice Marchand, meanwhile, had turned to face the courtroom and stood impassively with his arms folded.

"We will reconvene — how about an early start? 9:00 AM tomorrow?"

There were no objections.

Forty-five minutes later, His Honor was locking his car at a parking lot by the SkyDome. Another dollop of chance? Well, maybe: it was the *last* space in the lot! Tom wasn't all that keen about leaving his car there. Just across the fence lay the remains of rubble from a demolished building. The workmen clearing it were on lunch. It meant dust and dirt, but to find another spot to park would also mean missing the first inning. Tom opted for dust and dirt.

Two hours later he saw the consequence of his decision, but another helping of chance made it a minor issue. It had been a dull game and Tom had left in the bottom of the eighth to beat the rush. After unlocking his car — actually, it wasn't *too* dirty — he straightened to take off his wind-breaker, and there, not more than half a dozen paces away on the other side of the fence, was Whispering Hope! Any other time Tom would have paid little attention, but there was no ignoring or mistaking that huge gut.

Hope was standing by the wheel of a backhoe with two other men. The three were having one of those shouted conversations so typical of construction sites where the equipment noise makes communication difficult. Unlike Hope, his two companions — a lot younger, Tom noticed —

wore ear protectors, but they were pushed up above their ears. Walter Hope's hands were cupped behind his. His hard hat was white, too, Tom noticed, while the others' were yellow.

Whatever the subject of the conversation — it appeared to be a joke, for all three guffawed when it ended — the two younger men turned away to pick up shovels. Tom watched Hope hitch his hands under his mighty belly and swing up into the seat of the backhoe. The cover flap of the exhaust pipe, which had been barely vibrating before, now clattered away like a flag gone mad as the big man drove up the revs and poised the bucket to scoop some rubble. This was a man who loved to wrestle his machine.

Tom opened his car door finally, and sat in. He was depressed. Not only a lousy game, he thought, but — was it chance? — I've run into a witness.

"Now what do I do?" He was talking to the steering wheel without seeing it. "Do I speak to Ms. Dankert in chambers tomorrow? Talk to the kids' counsel too? Well, before anything, I'm going back to read that pretrial report again. If I go right now, it'll take me till just after the evening rush."

He started the car and waited patiently for the engine to warm. From the driver's seat he could see the car was dirtier than he'd first thought.

► *What will Tom Houghton be looking for in the pretrial report? What is bothering him that he feels he may have to bring up with the two attorneys?*

13

An Unlikely Place To Die

▼

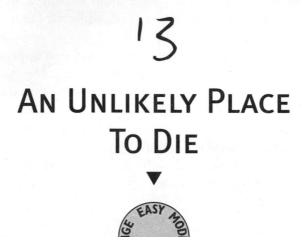

Because of the traffic, mostly the snarl at the underpass on Wolfe Road, Brad Matchett got to the scene an hour later than he'd said he would. A late afternoon thunderstorm yesterday, with high winds and heavy rain, had caused so many power outages that some traffic lights were still out, making the morning rush hour worse than usual. Normally, Brad would have slapped the red flasher on the roof and driven around the line of cars, but because of the underpass, he couldn't do that. To make matters worse, he'd then made a wrong turn. The big estates in Cedar Springs were set in a maze of crescents and cul-de-sacs and one-way streets designed to discourage all but the most committed drivers. He'd become so lost he was forced to call the dispatcher to find out where he was.

The only upside in this case so far, it occurred to Brad, if indeed there can be upsides for the head of a homicide division, was that being late wasn't really a disaster because an accidental death, even if drugs are involved, is not usually a light-flashing, siren-blaring matter. Unless of course the victim happens to be a *somebody*.

In this case, it was close. The victim was almost a somebody. Not quite, but almost. Mme Marie-Claude de Bouvère appeared from time to time on the social pages of *The Enterprise*. Not so much because she was the wife of the former Haitian ambassador; more because she was a one-time tennis star. Good enough for two cracks at Wimbledon in her teens. That made her status too close to call, so Brad had gone out himself just to be on the safe side.

Mme de Bouvère had been discovered shortly after sunrise by her gardener. The body lay in a gazebo set between the de Bouvères' huge house and their tennis court. On a table in the gazebo, along with her tennis racket, were all the appropriate paraphernalia for preparing and injecting a substance. Her tennis bag held three small bags of white powder. Brad knew all this from Sergeant Willy Peeverdale who, until Brad managed to get there, was the investigating officer in charge. For now, that was the extent of his information because the underpass on Wolfe Road had cut off radio communication. Now, almost an hour later, Brad was finally turning into a circular drive that looped the huge property at 23 Serene Crescent.

The property was very private. So were all the estates in Cedar Springs. A screen of sycamores and magnolias lined Serene Crescent so that even the most intrepidly curious driver would never see the house. Just to be sure, another screen, Colorado blue spruce this time, duplicated the effort about fifty paces behind the other trees. Interesting, Brad noted. Not one cedar.

Had it not been for the yellow crime-scene tape on the

south side of the house, he would have spent yet more time looking for the gazebo, but the tape led him through a grove of honey locust and along a path of brick chips to the back of the house. The property here was even larger than the front. The gazebo, big as it was — to Brad it looked more like the band shell in Misty Meadows Park — appeared almost lonely and curiously out of place. It sat precisely midway between the house and the tennis court, completely surrounded by a perfectly manicured lawn.

"Nothin's touched, but we gotta move fast 'cordin' to the coroner" The voice behind him made Brad jump. He would never get used to Peeverdale's habits. The sergeant made no small talk, ever. He never said "hello"; he never said "excuse me." And if he was aware that he made people nervous by suddenly appearing behind them, he'd never made any effort to change.

Peeverdale pressed on. "Says she can confirm the drug thing better the sooner she gets into the postmortem. Figures death occurred between ten and eleven last night. Sure looks like they OD'd. The guy died first she thinks, but only by a bit."

"The guy? They?" Brad realized he was sounding excited.

"Yeah." Peeverdale was never flapped either. "Guess that didn't come through on your radio. Y'see, the gardener, he saw Maa-daam de . . . de . . . whatever . . . lyin' there in that thing, that gay-zee-bo, and he split for the phone. Waited for us in the driveway. We found the guy. Figure it's Mister . . . Mon-*soor* de Boov . . . Boo . . . I can't get the doggone name right! Anyway we found him on the ground on the other side. Looks like he was sittin' on the rail and went over. For sure it's the missus on the floor, 'cordin' to the gardener. The guy's got no ID on him."

Sergeant Peeverdale dropped a pace behind Brad as they approached the gazebo, but continued talking. "Looks like the two of them were gonna play a little tennis last night. Or maybe they already played, it's hard to tell. And then they figured they'd get a little buzz on. My guess is they got some hot stuff they weren't expectin' and it did them in. "

There were two steps up into the gazebo, and Brad stopped on the first one to study the body of Mme de Bouvère lying flat on the floor. Well, not really flat. Reclining was more like it. The woman appeared so composed, so much an elegant study in white. Not a mark or a smudge or a speck on the white blouse or the white tennis skirt or the white sneakers. Except for the slight pinch to her eyes, it looked as though she had known she would be seen like this and had prepared for it.

Peeverdale, meanwhile, had not interrupted his monologue. "Gardener found her there at about 7:00 AM. Comes every other day to mow the lawn. S'pose that's why it looks like a billiard table. Mine sure don't look like this. Anyway, he came to get some equipment he left yesterday and noticed the lights on over the tennis court. That's when he saw Maa. . . her. He didn't see the guy. You gotta look over the rail to see him. Uh . . . the coroner, she wants us to hustle, Captain. It's the drug thing. Says the sooner the better."

"Tell you what, Peev," Brad said. "You give her a call. Tell her we'll be a while. We've got to figure out first where this lady died. And maybe the guy, too."

"You mean," Sergeant Peeverdale reached inside his tunic and scratched absently, "you don't think she died right here?

"No," Brad replied. "I don't."

► *Why does Brad Matchett think that Mme de Bouvère did not die at the gazebo?*

14

THE LAST WILL AND TESTAMENT OF NORVILLE DOBBS, ORTHOGRAPHER

▼

"Have you got lots of tissues too?" Amy Clumpus called to her receptionist. "This bunch will fake tears like nothing you have ever seen. Every one of them."

The receptionist had just rolled in the silver coffee service as Amy was arranging seven chairs at precisely equal distances from the big oak desk.

"Come to think of it, bandages wouldn't be a bad idea either," Amy said to herself. "When this will gets read there'll be some wrist slashing, for sure."

The last will and testament of Norville Dobbs, Orthographer, was to be read that morning in the office of the senior partner of Clumpus, Clumpus, and Loretto, and Amy was prepared for battle. She knew the contents of the will would not please very many in the family. In fact, she felt that anything short of complete hysterics this morning might be a treat.

The seven chairs were to be occupied shortly by Dobbs' two sisters, Adelaide and Adeline, and his three sons, Lamont, Telford, and Bernard, as well as by Grace, the cook and housekeeper, and Jeurgens, the chauffeur, butler, gardener, and jack of all trades. None of them, Amy mused, would be pleasant company even in happy circumstances. The sisters hated their nephews, each other, and life. Of the three sons, two were complete dissolutes and the third a greedy and lazy ne'er-do-well. Grace was widely suspected of bringing about the early demise of Norville Dobbs, Orthographer, by means of her cooking. Only Jeurgens, always dull, seemed harmless.

Amy made one last adjustment to the chairs. Such a contrast they were to old Dobbs himself, she thought. Gentle and unselfish, Dobbs had been born with only two passions. One was studiously ignoring the tons of money his father had left him, the other was correct spelling. To the latter, except for a brief pause to marry and father three sons, he had devoted not only his entire life, but also — and here was the crunch, Amy knew — the bulk of his estate.

"They're here!" The receptionist's voice on the speaker made Amy jump, but she recovered herself in time to nod graciously at the seven as they filed in to the carefully positioned chairs. Amy wanted to get it over with.

"Normal procedure," she said, "is for me to read the entire will. If you have any questions, you can ask them when I have read the whole thing. Okay?"

"Well, not quite." It was sharp-eyed Bernard, who held an envelope in his hand. "You don't have the will. We do."

Amy's eyes narrowed.

"Yes," Bernard continued. "We know you have a will there on your desk, but this is a newer one. Father made it out the day before he died. It's witnessed by all of us, even Jeurgens. See? And see the date?"

Amy took it from him but she struggled to keep her hands from shaking. It was a newer will, all right. Bernard went on.

"You recognize that stupid old Underwood of Father's, don't you?"

Amy acknowledged that the typing had certainly been done on Norville's creaky old machine with the raised *e* and the missing crossbar on the *t*.

"And that's his signature. You've seen it often enough." There was no question that the signature was either Norville Dobbs's or the best forgery Amy had seen in her years as a lawyer.

"So," Bernard said smugly. "Read. We know what's in it. He told us. But you read it. We want to be legal, you know."

Amy began to read out loud, slowly:

I, Norville Dobbs, Orthographer, being of sound mind do hereby declare the contents of this will shall super-cede all other wills and testaments signed by me before this date, and further declare that the contents of this will shall be read upon my death and that the contents of my estate be distributed as follows:

Amy paused and looked at Bernard, then at the others. "You've all signed this willingly?"

Each of them nodded.

"And you realize that by signing it, you declare that you saw Norville himself sign it?"

Again nods.

"Well, I'm not going to let you get away with it."

► *What did Amy find to make her suspect fraud?*

15

NOT YOUR AVERAGE HARDWARE STORE

▼

"So you think that's why we were handed this one?" Gordon Pape's question was rhetorical. He really didn't expect an answer but got one anyway.

"Figure it," Hugh Furneaux said. "Why else would the agency bring us this far north? It can't be any other reason. They've more than enough bodies up here for this kind of work."

"This kind of work," on this particular morning, was a repossession. Gordon Pape and Hugh Furneaux worked for SIMM Resolutions, a collection agency. "Field operatives," they were called in the agency's pretentious terminology, the ones who actually went out to face the locked doors, the insults, the angry dogs, the tears, even on occasion — and by far the most disturbing — sad, silent acceptance. All in order to repossess unpaid merchandise.

"My God. Look at it!" Hugh Furneaux exclaimed. "He must be a character all right."

The two operatives had pulled off the road to park in front of an ugly cement-block building. Its large yellow and black sign proclaimed it to be:

"A Real Man's Hardware Store."

Hugh scanned the shopworn banners in the display windows that flanked the front door. "Hard to believe there aren't some feminists out picketing here," he said. "I could see their point, too!"

The banners, all of them as dusty as the goods in the display windows, each supported Wilfrid Norman's idea of what a real hardware store must be, or a real *man's* hardware store at any rate.

"Real Men Don't Buy Teacups," one said.

Another offered:

"You Want *Seven* of Something. Ask Us!"

And directly underneath:

"No Pre-Packaging! We Sell You What You Want!"

Still another announced:

**"If We Ain't Got It,
Then It Ain't Hardware!"**

The **"ware"** had partly torn off from the end of the last banner and hung away from its host sentence at an awkward angle.

"You know," Hugh observed to his partner, "it may not just be that we're strangers. This guy could be very hard-nosed. Did you see that big shepherd running loose out back in the storage area? I'll bet he didn't come with a 'Good with Children' guarantee. Wonder if there's another loose inside?"

Gordon Pape was about to reply but then paused. He was looking at the Christmas lights that hung from the fluorescent fixtures just behind the windows. In mid-July. Apparently Wilfrid Norman's sole concession to the festive season was to plug and unplug an extension cord.

"I was here once," he said absently. "Needed a new handle for my splitting maul up at the cottage."

"Your *what*?" For the first time since they'd pulled in, Hugh took his eyes off the front of Norman's hardware store and looked directly at Gordon.

"A spli— Never mind. Not important," Gordon said. "The point is, the guy had one here. In stock. Actually he had about half a dozen! You just don't buy that kind of thing in a typical hardware store anymore. That's one of those crummy special orders that takes forever and gets surcharged to boot, all because some bean counter has told the owner his inventory has to roll over a certain number of times a year."

"And the whole place is like that," Gordon continued. "Full of everything you'd never get anywhere else. It's dirty and it's dusty and it's scattered all over the store. There's bins, barrels, shelves. Don't know how anybody can find anything, but they do. Well, anyway he does. Norman, I mean. He paused reflectively for a moment. "It's really your good old-fashioned hardware store. Everybody for miles around knows it."

"That's what I meant about why we were asked to do this," Hugh commented. "All the SIMM people up here must know him. That's why we're here to pick up — what is it anyway? It's a computer isn't it?" He reached into the back seat for a clipboard. "Yeah. Kirznet Cash Flow Control System."

He looked out at the display windows again. "Somehow it just doesn't seem to fit in there, does it?"

Gordon chuckled. "Probably why he hasn't paid for it."

"Well, pay or not," Hugh opened the car door, "let's get it over with." He was halfway out the door and then sat down again. "By the way, I make it 9:15. Is that what you've got? Awfully late for an old-fashioned hardware store to still be closed."

"That's true," Gordon replied, a note of concern in his voice. The two men got out and stood beside their car to take in a wider view. The area was very quiet. There was no one else around.

The "Real Man's Hardware Store" had no sidewalk in front of it, just a small parking lot, empty this morning. There were no adjacent stores either; the building was separated from the edge of town by a small field.

"This isn't a holiday or something, is it?" Hugh looked at Gordon as they approached the front door. "Don't they have a half-holiday or something like that in these little towns when everybody closes."

"Not in the morning," Gordon said, somewhat distractedly for they'd reached the door and it was definitely locked.

"Wow! Look at that latch!" Hugh said. "This has to be the last store in the country with a thumb la— Oh, oh! Look there."

"I see it — him," Gordon answered.

On the floor inside, just a few steps from the door, the body of a man lay face down at an angle slightly oblique to the door. Hugh and Gordon moved to the display windows on either side so they could peer in.

The body was that of a man at the far end of middle age. They could see white hair protruding over the edge of a baseball cap, some of the tufts leading to the back of his lined neck. He wore a red smock, the kind one might normally expect on a hardware store clerk.

The position of the body seemed peculiar. It lay in a very wide pool of blood that seemed to have congealed at the edges now. The man's legs were crossed at the ankles as though he had tripped himself and fallen that way. One hand, his left, was in the pocket of his shiny brown pants. The other was in the small of his back, palm upward. In the wan light from the fluorescents left on for night-time security, both Hugh and Gordon noted its soft, clean, whiteness in contrast to the menace just above it. For there, inches above the hand, thrust deep into the man's back, was a black-handled knife, a multi-purpose sportsman's knife, probably one from the store. It appeared as though the victim's last living effort had been to try to pull it out.

Neither Hugh nor Gordon felt an urge to rush. There was no question the man was dead and had been for some time.

"I'll call," Hugh said, pulling himself back from the scene. "Do they have 9-1-1 here?"

"They must," Gordon replied. "Wouldn't matter anyway. Everybody knows Wilfrid Norman's place."

"Sure, but that's not Wilfrid Norman," Hugh said over his shoulder on the way to the car and the cellular phone.

► *Gordon Pape has been to Wilfrid Norman's store before, and might recognize the hardware man, but how does Hugh Furneaux know that the dead man is not Wilfrid Norman?*

16

WHO HID THE MEDICINE?

▼

"When we have the first answer, we'll probably get the second too. Or vice versa." Christian Hawkes passed the transmitter from his left to his right hand and turned his back to the little group at the far end of the conference room. He spoke more softly.

"The thing is, I'm not even sure whether this is attempted murder or just mischief. Well, *stupid* mischief. Anybody who'd hide someone's medication like that is either malicious or bananas. Over."

The two questions to which Corporal Christian Hawkes of the RCMP was seeking answers were: who had hidden Kelly O'Miara's asthma medication in an air duct high in the wall of the Territories Room at the Mountain Lake Conference Centre, and why had he or she done it?

"Are you okay?" The voice on the other end of the

conversation wanted to know. "Is everything under control now? Over."

"Yes, everything is fine now," Christian replied. "The road is not open officially yet but you can see the odd car now without four-wheel drive, and the weather is certainly clear."

Christian had come to the Mountain Lake Centre at dawn two hours before, via snowmobile because the road had been closed and unplowed owing to avalanche warnings. He was the only person at headquarters able to respond when the manager of Mountain Lake had radioed for help just before midnight. What had been needed was medication for Kelly O'Miara, who had been having an asthmatic attack, or, failing that, an ambulance or helicopter to take her to the hospital. But weather and the closed road had ruled all that out, so Christian, with his paramedic qualifications and snowmobile expertise, was the next best choice.

"In fact," Christian was still talking, "it was all in hand by the time I got here. The manager found her medication when the cover to the air duct fell off. Whoever stuck it back on did a lousy job. She just got the Ventilin in time apparently, and she is all right now."

He changed the hand holding the transmitter again. "Look. I've got to go. They're getting antsy to leave, and if we've really got a crime here I'm going to have to find out yes or no in the next few minutes. If the road opens send a truck for me and the snowmobile. I'll call you in an hour. Over and out."

Christian set the little transmitter into its cradle and walked to the other end of the long, narrow Territories Room with studied casualness. The customary sensitivity he knew was essential for interrogation was going to be especially important here. The suspect— if there really was a suspect — would be one of the group of disabled people clustered around the sideboard that took up one wall of the alcove.

They were militants, the manager had said. "Chewy" was the word he'd used to describe them. "Didn't seem to like anything or anybody."

As he approached them, Christian looked at Perky Hinton sitting calmly in her wheelchair. She seemed confident. And well she might be, he thought. It probably wasn't her; she couldn't reach that high.

Perky, as though she could read his mind, piped up:

"It wasn't me. I can't reach up there. Besides, what would I want to hurt Kelly for? I didn't even know her till yesterday. I've got nothing against her."

"None of us knew anyone before, you nit." It was Val Horst. He held his white cane well out in front of him. "None of us knew . . ."

"I don't like this," a voice complained, just a bit wheezily. It was the older man that Christian had noticed before, rocking back and forth slightly on an overstuffed ottoman that was really too low to be comfortable. The man spoke very deliberately. One word at a time. "I don't like this at all. It's just like the institution. Too much arguing. I don't like the arguing."

"It's all right," Christian said. "No one is accusing anyone yet." He turned to the two remaining gentlemen. The manager had made a special point of describing these two when he'd first arrived. Homer and Harry were identical twins, both deaf and so similar in appearance that had not Homer been wearing hearing aids, no one could have possibly distinguished him from Harry.

Christian looked at Homer and simultaneously using sign language, he said out loud:

"Are you the twin with speech?"

"Yes." Homer replied in the slow, careful modulation of the deaf. Like Christian he signed at the same time. "Sometimes I help my brother. He doesn't talk. But that doesn't matter because everybody here can sign. You have to. It's part of the deal."

Harry nodded vigorously, and rapidly signed that he was pleased that Christian could sign too.

Perky's voice broke in. "Even if you didn't, officer, it wouldn't matter. Harry can read lips just about better than anyone.

Harry smiled, proud of himself. Then his face grew serious, and he signed to Christian. "I didn't put the medicine in the air duct. And my brother Homer didn't either. We couldn't have. We were in our room the whole time."

Val Horst snorted. "You were down here yesterday afternoon at five o'clock because you came in when the five o'clock news was on the radio. That is hardly being in your room the whole time."

"I'm afraid that's right, Mr. Hawkes," Perky Hinton added. "That's the time I saw them too. But that doesn't mean they hid the drugs."

"No, it doesn't, Perky," Christian replied. "But it's already obvious that there's someone here who is not being completely truthful. Maybe if we get that cleared up first, we'll get to the bottom of this caper."

► *Of whom is Christian suspicious, and why?*

17

SHOULD THE THIRD
SECRETARY SIGN?

▼

H ad she been more of a feminist, Ena Mellor would likely
have raised Cain, or at least been resentful, over the fact
that last spring's round of promotions had gone exclusively to
men. But she wasn't particularly intense about her
feminism; nor was she the type to hold a grudge. Besides,
she'd gotten a bit of a prize in any case. Her rank may
have continued to be Third Secretary, which she'd been for
the past two years, but now she was Third Secretary at the
embassy in Vienna instead of in Cairo.

For Ena the transfer meant an apartment in which the
plumbing worked as a rule and not an exception. There was
no *baksheesh* to pay every time she needed anything done.
She could picnic in the grounds of the Schonbrunn Palace
with no beggars playing on her guilt. There were concerts —
oh, were there concerts! Mozart, Beethoven, Mahler . . . And

museums. And churches. And history. Ena knew that if she had pushed hard last spring, she might have become a Second Secretary, but in Katmandu. Hard to get good schnitzel in Katmandu. No, Third Secretary in Vienna was definitely a better deal.

Admittedly, the Soviets had messed up her pleasure temporarily. When their tanks rolled into Prague last month and forced Alexander Dubcek and the Czech government to accept "normalization," a flood of refugees had spilled into Austria. Most of them ended up in the Traiskirchen camp. Among other things, the location of the camp interrupted Ena's now thoroughly established habit of lunching at one of the street cafes in St. Stephen's Square. Still, Traiskirchen wasn't all that bad, for it was set in a vineyard near the city.

What bothered Ena a lot more was making decisions that deeply affected the lives of the refugees. Her signature at the bottom of a single document could mean freedom for a refugee. Without her signature, the applicant could well be sent back to the repression behind the Iron Curtain. It was a power that made Ena Mellor extremely uncomfortable.

Well over half the refugees had no papers, for they'd fled that night of August 21 with only the clothes on their backs. Ena often had to rule on the truth of an applicant's identity on the basis of a driver's license, or a photograph, or a work card. Yesterday, the only proof one refugee could offer was the few koruny in her purse.

The man who sat before her now offered her a first, however. He had no passport — nothing unusual about that for someone from behind the Iron Curtain — no driver's license, no work card, in fact, nothing but a very worn and creased photograph. Nevertheless, it was a photograph that certainly suggested his life would be in danger if he were returned to Czechoslovakia, and police officials there knew he was coming.

The picture had been taken in Moscow. Even without Ena's experience in foreign affairs, she would have recognized Red Square and the Lenin Mausoleum. It took a magnifying glass, however, to see that the man in front of the Mausoleum was also the man sitting nervously on the other side of her desk. The same glass showed, very clearly, that he was vandalizing one of the USSR's most important monuments by painting over Lenin's name. Most noticeable was that the "L" had been changed to a box, and the "I" had been altered to resemble a Byzantine cross. How he had accomplished this in the middle of Red Square, with all the guards about, was incomprehensible to Ena, but it was a crime that, if he'd been caught, would have meant a long stretch in a *gulag*. Still, how he'd done it was not Ena's problem. Her problem was whether or not to sign his application. She could see that he was trying to put one over on her, but then it could be that he was just another desperate refugee.

► *What has Ena noticed that makes her think he is "trying to put one over on her"?*

18

THE CASE OF THE JEWELRY THIEVES

▼

The twice-daily bus from Lindeville made only two stops in the straight run due east from Benton. The first was on the edge of Lindeville itself, right at the point where two used-car dealerships bracketed the highway, and brought Lindeville to a close with huge signs that promised fair deals, square deals, and no money down. The second was about five minutes farther out, in a sparsely populated rural area at the midway point between the two towns. For years the bus company had tried to establish several more stops. The highway was too desolate, it argued, too subject to chilling winds in winter and overwhelming heat in summer. But the highways department steadfastly refused. Too disruptive of traffic, the officials claimed, and precedent setting as well. If it were done for the stretch from Lindeville to Benton, it would have to be done for the other three directions too.

So every night the pride of the Lindeville Tour, Transport, and Travel fleet — a former Greyhound Dreamliner, its dreams long since fulfilled and forgotten — lumbered out to the car dealerships, where it paused in a ragged symphony of air brakes and diesel coughs to discharge some morose passenger, and then continued on to what locals called the "nowhere stop" before delivering its charges to Benton and points beyond.

The old bus was making the first of these two stops as Steve Fleck of the Lindeville Constabulary pulled around it and accelerated down the highway and out of town. He felt stuffy and uncomfortable in the patrol car; the heater worked properly only on high, and he'd been in the car for two hours now. That afternoon around 4:00, just before what passed as Lindeville's rush hour, four armed robbers had hit Zonka Jewelry Ltd. in a lightning swoop. Very professional, or at least very experienced, they had stripped the cash register, the display cases and even the small safe where Zonka's kept its Christmas layaway sales. Steve had been in the patrol car when the burglar alarm sounded in the station, but even though he had headed for Zonka's with red light flashing and siren blaring — both of which he hated with a passion — the thieves were well clear by the time he got there.

It had been a carefully planned event. To Steve it appeared almost rehearsed, as it may well have been, for as witnesses described it, the robbers were in and out in only a few minutes, with one man at the door, a second and third gathering the stock, and a fourth at the wheel of a car outside. The timing had been precise in every way. There was usually a lull in the store's customer traffic at that point of the day, and the inventory at Zonka's was at its peak, what with Christmas only a week away. The getaway car had bolted into Lindeville's downtown streets just before traffic began to build.

In fact there were really only two things that Steve Fleck could feel good about. One was that he had a good description of the robbers' car: a blue Honda LX, somewhat dirty from the winter roads, with a very obvious dent in the right rear fender. Actually, that part made Steve uneasy. These guys were so professional; yet it almost seemed they wanted their car to be remembered.

The other good thing — Steve felt pretty sure it was a good thing — was that the robbers were still in Lindeville somewhere. They had to be. They may well have been very smooth, but Steve and his colleagues were no slouches themselves. There were only four roads out of town and they had been blocked immediately. Now the roadblocks had been lifted to tempt the robbers out of hiding.

The Lindeville Constabulary was keeping a careful watch on every road, but so far there was no evidence that the getaway car had left town, and a nagging concern was beginning to develop that maybe the enterprising gang had slipped out of town after all.

Steve was quite far ahead of the pride of the Lindeville Tour, Transport, and Travel fleet, so he spotted the passenger at the highway stop a minute or so before the bus would arrive. Half on impulse, half deliberately, he pulled over to the rickety old bus shelter.

"I'm going to Benton," he said. "To the outskirts anyway. It's too hot in here, but at least you don't have to breathe diesel fumes if you ride with me."

The passenger flashed him a warm smile. It was a young woman. "Oh thanks! I was freezing! I'm afraid to hitchhike. There's only been a couple of cars going toward Benton anyway." She got in and immediately began unwrapping the scarf that was drawn tightly over her head.

Steve was very nonchalant. "You didn't happen to, uh . . . notice any of the cars, did you? Like . . . uh . . . new cars or old?" He could hear the bus coming now and glanced in the rearview mirror, to make sure it was stopping, before he pulled onto the highway.

"No." She gave him a warm smile again. "I really don't know much about cars. One was a Japanese car, though, a blue one. They're easier to tell, don't you think? The Japanese cars?" She folded the scarf in her lap. "Anyway, this one had a banged-in fender. That's why I noticed."

Steve slowed and pulled over onto the shoulder of the road. The bus pulled past them, accelerating down the highway in a barrage of noise and noxious fumes.

"What's the matter? What are you doing?" The young lady was frightened. "Why are you stopping? Is this a trick? You're making me miss the bus!" She was almost in tears.

"Miss, we're just going to sit here for a minute," Steve said, "and watch the road until you tell me who you are and where you've been today."

► *Steve Fleck's must think this would-be bus passenger to Benton has something to do with the robbery. Why?*

19

THE MURDER OF
MR. NORBERT GRAY

▼

Jim Latimer hung up the phone. "That was F.A.R.," he said. From his desk across the overcrowded squad room, Mike Roslin nodded absently. He was staring at an open evidence bag.

"Thought so," he acknowledged finally. "And don't tell me. The Beretta's hers, right?"

"Uh huh." Jim Latimer nodded. "Registered in 1984, uh, let's see, on March fifteenth. No, the sixteenth. Firearm Registration's got data on disk back to 1986. Anything before that they gotta dig out by hand. That's what took 'em so long to call back."

Mike Roslin rubbed his elbow back and forth along the arm of his chair. "And the Luger?" he asked, picking a deadly looking weapon out of a holster that bore the double lightning bolts of the SS on the cover flap.

"His. Registered the same day. They bought both guns at Intutus Firearms Shop on Mount Pleasant. Luger's registered for range use. The Beretta can be carried."

"Humpf." Mike was clearly unimpressed. He began to invert the evidence bag over his desk.

"Wait!" His partner shouted so loud that the two other detectives in the room rose out of their chairs. "You know what happened the last time we used your desk!"

The others chuckled and went back to their work. Mike Roslin had a reputation as the best problem-solver on the homicide squad, but one whose desk, locker, car, and apartment were so covered in flotsam that even he no longer knew what he owned.

"Here," Jim directed. "Dump it on my desk. Then at least we'll know which murder we're trying to solve."

Without a word, Mike carried the bag around to his partner's desk and slowly eased the contents onto the surface. Except for the Luger and its holster, both nestled in the pile of incomplete reports, empty coffee cups, and Mr. Submarine wrappers on Mike's desk, the story of Norbert Gray's untimely demise now lay spread out on Detective Jim Latimer's desk blotter.

Just forty-eight hours ago, Norbert Gray had been shot in the back of the head while sitting at the solid oak rolltop in his den. After an acrimonious and very public divorce from his wife of seventeen years, Gray had been living alone in their custom-built log home in the exclusive Pines district. The ex-wife, Aleyna, was in custody, but not yet formally charged.

There had been one shot at close range from a 9 mm Beretta. Apparently, the shooter — the evidence pointed overwhelmingly at this being the former Mrs. Gray — had stood behind the victim, fired once, and then threw the gun out the balcony doors. It had skidded down the side of the ravine that backed onto the Gray home, and come to rest (lucky for the investigators) against a tree trunk at the edge of a bike path. The techs had quickly determined that the Beretta was indeed the murder weapon, and that it had a single fingerprint on it. At the end of the barrel, curiously, but a clear print nevertheless. More to the point, the print belonged to Aleyna Gray.

The Beretta lay in the center of the pile on Jim Latimer's desk. Mike stuck the eraser end of a pencil inside the trigger guard and absently spun the little gun in circles.

"Something really stinks about all this," he said.

"Yeah," Jim nodded. "You said that yesterday. And this morning too."

"Well, it does," came the reply. "I don't like these near-smoking-gun cases."

This time it was Jim who used a pencil to play with the evidence. "Yeah, but . . ." He stuck the point under an envelope and flipped it over so that Norbert Gray's name and address looked up at them. "There's two of these letters," he said. "Both from her. The one from two weeks ago tells him what a jerk he is, how inadequate he is, what a lousy father, worse as a husband. Sure glad I never had to tangle with this woman. The second one, it's what? Three days before the murder? Tells him what she'd like to do to him."

"Okay, but . . ." Mike took the pencil out of the Beretta's trigger guard and tapped the postal mark and then the stamp on first one letter, then the other. "Personal letters, sure. But everything's typed. WordPerfect, I'd say, and a laser printer. Lots of those around."

"Then what about the will?" Jim asked. Norbert Gray's will had been found on the surface of the rolltop. A line had been drawn through the clauses relating to Aleyna, but there was no signature or initialing near it.

"Sure, what about it? Watch this." Jim winced in disbelief as Mike drew a line across a report lying on Jim's typewriter. "Doesn't tell us a thing!" Mike continued.

"And the cigarettes?" Jim asked the question in almost a whisper. He was still staring at the report.

"Easy to set up. He didn't smoke. She does." Mike pointed a finger at a half-empty pack on the desk. "Yes, it's her brand. Yes, her prints are on the pack, but look, this is garbage. It's all circumstantial."

Jim finally took his eyes off the report. "Still, she sure had motive," he said. "Hated the guy, at least according to the transcript of the divorce. And she's got no alibi: 'I had a cold and took some aspirins and went to bed early.' Pretty weak."

"On the other hand," Mike replied, "we have no eye-witness, and there's really nothing solid here. Look, I'm not on her side, but maybe somebody's setting her up. Maybe somebody's setting *us* up!" He picked up the evidence bag. "All a good lawyer has to do is show that one of these pieces of evidence is phony and the whole lot goes out the window!"

"Yeah." Jim picked up the destroyed report tenderly. "What we need is something like DNA."

Mike looked at his partner. He became so animated that Jim moved to protect his cup of coffee. "That's it!" Mike shouted. "We can use DNA to prove one of these pieces of evidence is solid — or phony, for that matter! At least then we'll know if we have a real case or not."

The excitement affected Jim as he too caught the idea. "Yes! DNA!" He reached across the desk, and as he grabbed the evidence bag, a large, grayish-white wad fell out of it. "What's this?" He peered hard at his partner. This wasn't in here before!"

Mike looked perplexed. "Looks like my sock."

"What's it doing in the evidence bag?" Jim asked.
"I dunno."

► *What, in the evidence the two detectives have, can be subjected to DNA testing?*

20

SOME UNCERTAINTY ABOUT THE CALL AT 291 BRISTOL

▼

There were at least three good reasons why Shaun Hawkes was not prepared to accept the incident at 291 Bristol as a break and enter. Not as a robbery either, or an assault, even though all that had to be put aside for the moment while she looked after the young woman who'd called 9-1-1. Paige Kress was her name, eighteen years old and by all indications genuinely traumatized. In Shaun's mind it was a heck of a thing to happen to a young college kid on her Christmas break, so she was now puttering about the huge kitchen at 291 Bristol, looking for the wherewithal to brew a pot of tea, Shaun's standard response to trauma, illness, and global crisis.

"He was gonna, I was so scared he was gonna . . ." Paige's first words to Shaun degenerated into moans as she wrapped her arms around herself tightly and rocked back and forth.

"He was here before, the guy. Like, in the house . . ." had come through the tears. "See, we're gonna move . . . Daddy's company's got some kind of trouble . . . and he needs to . . . to . . ." Paige had begun to hyperventilate. That's when Shaun had left for the kitchen. She wanted to make some space for herself, and tea for all hands.

Two of the uniforms on her squad were sitting with Paige right now, one of them the only other female member of the squad, a veteran of all of six months who had been the first officer on the scene. This same rookie, a month before, had investigated a report of three girls being stalked on the campus of the junior college nearby. One of the three had been Paige Kress.

The third cupboard door to the left of the triple sink yielded an electric tea kettle. Progress.

"Add that to the milk," Shaun said aloud, "and the dubious contents of that sugar bowl, and we're getting somewhere. Now, what's needed is a nice Darjeeling or maybe a Pekoe."

The search went on. A second bank of cupboard doors presented an impressive array of serving dishes and baking tools but no tea, so she moved to the third. Actually, this was taking about as much time as she had hoped it would. Paige, in Shaun's opinion, needed some time before telling her story again. The first time, between the sobs and fits of quivering, and even a near-faint, Paige had told the officers how she had just stepped out of the shower when she heard — she was certain about this — she heard a sound in the hall. Wrapped in only a towel, Paige had peeked out the door, but saw nothing. It was when she had turned back inside that she saw the intruder in the mirror: a man, a short man, dressed all in black, carrying a painting. She'd screamed, locked the door, and called 9-1-1.

"Ah, gotcha!" Shaun's delight at finally finding some

tea was short-lived. It was a herbal tea. Mint. In her opinion, that was as close to barbaric as one could get without resorting to coffee. This search for tea was becoming as bothersome as the case! Even the man in black had been easier to find.

Paige had identified him as the real-estate estimator who had been through the house the week before. He was now sitting in handcuffs in the back seat of a blue-and-white parked in the driveway. Shaun herself had picked him up only a block away.

She had to admit she disliked him immediately, probably because his black shirt was opened to mid-chest, revealing a cross on a gold chain, a St. Jude medal and, also in gold, a fist with middle finger raised in a rude gesture. He was short, dressed in black, and swaggery. Not Shaun's kind of person. Still, there had been no painting anywhere near; not that she'd expected to find one, even though the black Trans-Am where she'd picked him up was his. As well, his story that he'd returned to the neighborhood to re-evaluate his original estimate made sense enough. Paige's parents were selling their huge home and he'd been called in on the same day they were leaving for a week of skiing. His first go-round, he claimed, had been too rushed. The place needed a closer look, he went on. Too many things were not working: the garage-door opener, the burglar alarm, the garburetor. The house needed a thorough examination.

"Well," Shaun exclaimed as she opened and closed the very last cupboard door. "This is uncivilized! One cannot have a kitchen and not have tea! What do these people do for —"

With a look of chagrin on her face, she stopped and peeked over her shoulder to see if anyone had seen her search.

"Some detective!" she said, and walked to the sink. The set of canisters on the kitchen counter had labels clear enough to read from anywhere in the room: FLOUR, SUGAR, COFFEE, TEA. She peered out the kitchen door just to be doubly sure none of her squad had been nearby. Shaking her head in self-admonishment, she began to fill the kettle with water.

▸ *Shaun Hawkes almost overlooked the obvious in her search for tea, but she hasn't been fooled by this case. What are the "three good reasons" she is not prepared to accept this incident as break and enter, robbery, or assault?*

21

THE CASE OF THE STOLEN STAMP COLLECTION

▼

In the doorway of Mika Fleck's office stood a very nervous young man in a blue delivery uniform. Miles Bender was waiting to be summoned, and he wasn't the least bit comfortable about the idea.

Mika's opening statement didn't help either. "Come in here and sit down, young man," she said without looking up. "For heaven's sake you're going to wear out the rug with your fidgeting."

Miles shuffled across the floor to the only chair that was empty of books and files and all the paraphernalia of an extremely busy office. "It didn't get there, did it?" he said as he sat down. "The shipment. Like, the stamps?"

Mika looked over the top of her half-glasses, freezing Miles Bender in mid-squirm. "No," she said. "It did not. The first bonded shipment that Acceleration Courier Service has ever failed to deliver." She pushed up her glasses and looked through them. It didn't make Bender feel any more relaxed. "And I don't suppose you're surprised to know that collection is worth over half a million dollars. That's why we had a police escort."

"I know it was valuable." For the first time, Miles Bender stopped squirming. "I know that. But how can you blame *me* if the cops stole it. I mean — they looked like cops anyway."

Mika spread her hands on the desk and spoke more softly. "Okay. Let's go through it again. You say two policemen took the stamps. Just like that."

"Not just like that." Miles was beginning to whine in spite of Mika's obvious attempt to be more gentle with him. "I mean, they were cops! Look, it was standard procedure. All the way to the border, like, there were these two Vancouver city cops, one in front and one in back just the way we're supposed to do it. And at the border the two American cops took over, the ones from Bellingham. Motorcycle cops."

Miles Bender was becoming more confident as he sensed his side of the story was finally being listened to. He leaned forward in the chair. "I mean, there was no reason to be suspicious; you wouldn't have been either. They had real police bikes. Real uniforms — the boots, the gloves, the sunglasses, everything!"

Mika opened her mouth to speak, but Miles kept talking. "I mean they even *acted* like motorcycle cops. You know, sort of strutty and cocky and . . ."

"According to this report," Mika broke in, "you got a good look at them."

Miles took a deep breath. "At *one* of them, yeah. When we stopped on the highway and they made me get out. The one that put his bike in the van and, like, got in to drive, he got pretty close."

"According to your description," Mika said, "he is about

your height, but heavier. Bit of a beer belly. Blue eyes and a reddish moustache. Maybe thirty-five to forty years old."

"Yeah!" Miles Bender was enthusiastic in his agreement. "And the cut, the nick on his cheek? They got that on the report there? Like maybe he cut himself shaving?"

Mika nodded and then looked up from the report. "And you say all this took only a couple of minutes. They stopped. You stopped. They ordered you out, and then one of them put his bike in the van, and they took off leaving you at the side of the road."

"Exactly! That's it exactly!" Miles was excited now. "I mean, like, by this time I know they're not cops but, I mean, like, what am I gonna do?"

Mika cleared her throat. She was looking over the top of her glasses again. "For one," she said, "you're going to tell us where they took the stamps. Depending on how well you do that, we'll work out the next steps later."

▶ *Why is Mika Fleck suspicious of Miles Bender?*

22

THE CASE OF THE
BUCKLE FILE

▼

BEAVER LIFE & CASUALTY
INSURANCE COMPANY

1 October 1992

Mr. Ernie Buckle
104 West Fort William Road
Thunder Bay, ON
P8L V1X

Dear Mr. Buckle:

Re: Joint Life Policy BV 297562 – Ernie & Audrey Buckle

I have received your letter of 25 September 1992 and the
enclosed forms authorizing the addition to your policy of a

double indemnity clause for accidental death.

Please note that Mrs. Buckle has not signed Form 22A. Since yours is a joint policy with you and your wife as each other's beneficiary, it is necessary that both of you sign. Accordingly, I am returning Form 22A for her signature.

Further, you have not designated a beneficiary to receive the indemnity should it occur that you and Mrs. Buckle encounter a terminal accidental event together. The funds, if such were to occur, would thus be paid to your respective estates on a 50/50 basis, and would therefore be subject to probate fees and taxation. If this is your wish, you and Mrs. Buckle must initial clause 12 on page 2 of Form 22A. However, should you wish to designate a beneficiary, please enter his/her/their name(s) and address(es) in the space below clause 13 on page 2.

I will hold your cheque until I receive the completed Form 22A, and other instructions on the above matters.

Sincerely,

Christine Cooper

Christine Cooper
Client Services

Oct. 12/92

Beaver Insurance Co

Dear Miss Cooper,

Here is the form with my signature that you asked for. Sorry I didn't do this before. Ernie usually is the one who looks after these things. Also, like you said, for ~~beneficiair~~ beneficiary we picked my cousin Reenee Clubek in Gibralter.

Hope this is alright now.

Audie Buckle

BEAVER LIFE & CASUALTY
INSURANCE COMPANY

12 November 1992

Mr. Ernie Buckle
Mrs. Audrey Buckle
104 West Fort William Road
Thunder Bay, ON
P8L V1X

Dear Mr. and Mrs. Buckle:

Re: Joint Policy BV 297562

Enclosed please find notice of confirmation regarding changes to the above policy, with copies for your files.
   The changes are effective as of 15 October 1992.

Sincerely,

Jack Hal for Christine Cooper

Christine Cooper

July 29, 1993

Ms Christine Cooper
Beaver Life and Casualty

BY FAX

Your telephone message of 27/07/93 handed to me this AM. Body of Ernie Buckle recovered from Wabakimi Lake at

3:15 PM, 25/07/93. Coroner has ruled accidental death by drowning. No inquest scheduled.

Search for body of Audrey Buckle terminated this AM. Overturned canoe located in Wabakimi established as belonging to the Buckles. No further search planned. Status of Audrey Buckle is "presumed dead."

We will have full reports available by 10/08/93. You can get these through usual channels from district headquarters in Thunder Bay.

Constable Allan Longboat
Ontario Provincial Police
Search and Rescue Unit
Sioux Lookout

March 18, '94

To Whom It May Concern,
Beaver Life and Casualty Insurance
7272 Barton Street
Hamilton, Ontario
CANADA

VIA AIR MAIL

Dear Sir or Madam,
I am writing in regard to the deaths of Ernie and Audrey Buckle. As you know, I am the beneficiary named in the life insurance policy they held with your company.

Very shortly I will be moving from Gibralter to a project in east Africa. My new address, effective March 31, '94 will be:

c/o Central Postal Station
Box 241
Haile Selassie Blvd.
Nairobi 17
KENYA

It would be helpful if you could tell me when the policy benefit will be issued.

I appreciate your help in this matter.

Sincerely,

Irene Clubek

Irene Clubek

► *On April 2, 1994, Christine Cooper wrote a memo to her immediate superior stating that one item in particular made her feel that Beaver Life & Casualty was being defrauded in this case, and that the case might also involve a felony. What made her feel that?*

23

A Very Brief
Non-Interview

▼

The office was ultra modern, a place of hums. A hum came through the air-conditioning grate above the door. A double bank of fluorescent lighting hummed in the ceiling. Over in one corner, a 386 AT desktop hummed in droning, flat counterpoint to the spectacular, silent flowerbursts that looped in random delight on the screen.

Sheila Lacroix stood quietly in the midst of the hums. She could hear them, but paid no attention. There were too many other things to take in. The desk, just a few steps in front of her, was bulky, silent, imposing, and impeccably neat. Bookshelves on the wall to her left were filled with leather-bound volumes standing in silent, parade-ground readiness against the time when a user might have need of them. Below the shelves, a selection of newspapers was arranged carefully across a table. Sheila made a quick estimate; there were twenty different issues at least.

Across from her, and beyond the desk, the wall was glass from floor to ceiling, the panes set in almost invisibly narrow frames. She might have been on the twenty-second floor of any office building in New York, London, Geneva, or Toronto . . . Except for the newspapers. The New York and London *Times* were in the lineup all right, and out of the corner of her eye Sheila could see *Zeitung* on one of the mastheads. But the majority of the headlines were in Arabic. The view through the window told her where she was, too. Without moving her head, Sheila could count five of the mosques in central Amman.

But most especially, what told her — what would tell anyone — she was not in a Western country was the very tall man bending over a tiny table near the remaining wall. He was turned away from Sheila, and except for the hand resting on the back of his hip, an incredibly long index finger pointing at the windows, she could not see any part of him as he was entirely covered by his pristine white, flowing *thobe*, and over that a shorter *aba* in desert brown. The tall man, whose other hand was furiously signing documents, was Ibrahim Jamaa, leader of the Brotherhood of the Eternal Light of Allah. It was he whom Sheila Lacroix had come to see.

"Now don't stare at him, whatever you do!" Sheila could remember every one of the attaché's instructions clearly. "As a matter of fact, don't make eye contact at all, or for more than a second or two. He knows you're Western so he'll forgive you a glance, but . . .," he shrugged, "you're a woman. Hey, I don't make the rules! This is Jordan, not Saskatchewan."

It had struck Sheila at the time that the attaché was exceptionally world-weary for one so young. "I have no idea how you did this," the young man had said, shaking his head.

"No one — like, literally *nobody* — from any of the embassies has ever seen this guy close up; his organization is fanatical about secrecy — probably about a few other things, too! We've tried to get in here for months with no success, and   here he gives you an appointment just like that!" He lifted his hand to snap his fingers for emphasis but then decided such behavior would be undiplomatic.

Sheila wanted to point out quite firmly that a year of traveling and beating on doors and shouting and bribing and threatening was hardly "just like that." Fourteen months ago, her husband had been kidnapped, presumably for political reasons, somewhere in Haseke province in Syria, where the border meets Iraq and Turkey. Bill Lacroix was a doctor working there with Kurdish refugees. From the time of his disappearance until now, not a single one of the Middle Eastern groups known to use kidnapping for political purposes would acknowledge they held him.

Sheila had let the Canadian Department of External Affairs prove itself useless before striking out on her own. Since then, although she was only vaguely aware of it, she was probably the only Western non-diplomat and non-journalist to speak personally to the leadership of Black September, Hamas, the PLO, even the PPK. All of them had denied any knowledge of Bill Lacroix. Now Sheila was about to score the most significant coup of all, in the eyes of the diplomats anyway; she was about to speak directly to Ibrahim Jamaa of the Eternal Light of Allah.

"Don't speak first under any circumstances." The attaché had been full of advice. "You let him initiate the conversation. Somehow you've got to make it seem like you're answering *his* questions rather than the other way around."

"And . . . and . . ." The flow stopped suddenly. ". . . Uh . . . there's one more thing, Mrs. Lacroix, if you would?" For a few seconds, the attaché's diplomatic mask came off. "We . . . we know nothing about this Ibrahim Jamaa. We're not even absolutely sure what he looks like. One thing we know is that he's very tall. Unusually so, like, really basketball-tall! He wears a patch over his right eye; we know that. Speaks perfect English. Italian and German, too."

"So I'm supposed to bring you his birth certificate and his wedding album?" Sheila had long ago lost patience with External Affairs.

"No, no, no!!" The attaché reddened. "You see — and I'm being very frank with you here — what we have about him comes from the CIA and Mossad." He looked over Sheila's shoulder. "We really don't have a lot of faith in them anymore. So if there's anything that you see that is, well, *interesting*, we would like to know. Please?"

Sheila had taken one step into the elevator when he rushed to her and pulled her back gently. "One more thing we know. I don't really believe it would have anything to do with the whereabouts of Dr. Lacroix, but . . . Jamaa professes to be *mujtahid*. Means he's sort of a freethinker, especially about religion. Now the Shiites generally go along with that, but the Sunnis don't, and since Jordan is about eighty percent Sunni, that could make him a bit unwelcome here."

Standing in the office only a few minutes later, while Ibrahim Jamaa continued to write, helped Sheila understand all too well what it felt like to be unwelcome. However, when the man finally turned to face her, she forgot the feeling altogether. It was replaced by a sense of overwhelming menace that she knew would stay with her for a long time.

He was tall, all right, possibly seven feet, but that could be, Sheila later reflected, because of his power, his presence. Ibrahim Jamaa would have been a tower of malevolence at only six feet. He turned to her in what seemed like slow motion. First the patch appeared. Black, set in deep creases on the cheekbone. It was so striking that the rest of his face, Sheila was convinced, followed with abnormal slowness.

Despite herself, she stared. First at the patch, then at the single dark eye that appraised her without a flicker of response. Only when he brought his fingertips together in front of his chest — the incredibly long index finger had a matching partner — in what was just barely a gesture of greeting, did Sheila take her eyes away.

Jamaa took a step, then another. It brought him to the edge of the desk.

"Mrs. Lacroix," he said. Then there was silence. Sheila was suddenly aware of the hums again. She dared to glance up at the face and then looked down. The single eye still revealed nothing.

"Mrs. Lacroix," he said again. The attaché was correct about the English. Not a trace of an accent.

Sheila watched a long index finger as it tapped, first the edge of the desk, then the shoulder cradle attached to the telephone.

He appeared to be searching for the right words. The finger traced the slim, arching neck of a desk lamp. The man was clearly used to commanding long silences while others waited for him to speak.

"Your husband. . ."

Finally! The reason she was there! She was surprised the subject was broached so quickly.

"Your husband," he repeated. "The doctor. We have no interest in him. Our organization does not interfere with the work of medical relief. We seek only justice for true believers, the people who are thwarted in their search by the Zionist aggressors. I do not know where your husband is. The Brotherhood does not know where your husband is." Jamaa brought his fingertips together again in front of his chest and inclined his head ever so slightly. The interview — the *non*-interview — was over. He turned, slowly, and went back to the table where he had stood before.

Sheila had to pull her feet off the floor in order to turn and go out the door and across the hall to the elevators. She wasn't in the least surprised that the attaché got to his feet far more eagerly when the elevator doors opened than he had when they first met.

"What did you find out? What's he like?" He pressed in most undiplomatic style.

Sheila shook her head. "Nothing you'd be interested in. But it's a step ahead for me. The Brotherhood of the Eternal Light of Allah knows about my husband. They must."

"What makes you say that?" The young attaché was subdued, but curious.

"Because that was not Ibrahim Jamaa. Or if it was — which I doubt — that was not his office."

▶ *What has led Sheila Lacroix to this conclusion?*

24

A Clean Place to Make an End of It

▼

W hat intrigued Bob Gibson — bothered him, actually — was how *clean* the inside of the car was. Someone, quite possibly the dead woman herself, had vacuumed the interior rugs with special care. There wasn't a speck of dust anywhere on the dash, either, or along the steering column; even the short stalks behind the knobs on the radio had been wiped. The leather cover over the gearshift box had been cleaned of the dust and grit that always collect in the creases. That had taken a wet cloth or a chamois, Bob realized. So the cleaning was not just a casual, spontaneous effort.

It wasn't a new car. From where he was leaning into it, with both fists pressed into the driver's seat, Bob peered a little closer at the odometer. The light wasn't all that good in the little garage, and the car had been backed in so that the waning winter daylight from the open garage door came through the windshield directly into his face. Still, he could make out the figures: 47,583. No, not a new car at all. But one in great shape.

Bob leaned across the seat and, with the tip of his index finger, ticked the switch on the armrest to lower the passenger window just a bit. He checked to see if the earnest young policeman at the door had noticed, but he hadn't. If he had, and objected, Bob would have argued. The smell in the car was nauseating, and he needed to relieve it by letting a bit of draft through.

It was a smell he'd encountered before. Not so often as to be familiar with it. Maybe a half-dozen times or so in the past thirty years, but after the first time he'd never forgotten. It was the smell of a body in the early stages of decomposition: a hint of sweet and a hint of foul. Sickening.

The smell clung, too. The garage door had been open for several hours, ever since the body had been discovered earlier, around noon. But the whole building was still filled with the odor, and Bob knew it would be a long time before the fabric in the car would be free of it.

Inside the car, of course, it was worse. The doors had been open only long enough for the photographer to do her grisly job, and then again when the coroner removed the body. Bob was here to tow away the car to the police pound.

Over his years as owner of Palgrave Motors, Bob had come to know the police very well and he was the one they invariably called in situations like this. Therefore it was not, as he had reflected only seconds before, the first time he had been called to the scene of a suicide. Nevertheless, although all he had to do was take away the car, the whole business gave him the creeps.

According to the coroner, the woman — Bob didn't know her name — had backed the car into the little garage some forty to fifty hours ago, closed the door and simply sat there with the motor running until the inevitable happened. The body had gone unnoticed for almost two days, the coroner estimated.

"You didn't touch anything, did you?"

It was Officer Shaw. Bob hadn't heard him come in. The young policeman had been left behind by the investigating detective with specific and stern instructions that nothing was to be disturbed. Shaw took the order seriously.

Bob looked at him, uncertain just how to put his suspicions. He pointed to the two-way radio in Shaw's belt.

"Can you call your sergeant on that?"

Shaw didn't answer; he just looked at Bob curiously.

"Cause I think he'll want to take another look at all this," the older man said. "Missed something, I think."

► *Why has Bob Gibson drawn this conclusion?*

25

Murder at the David Winkler House

▼

Chris Beadle passed in the narrow hallway and looked back at the doorway she'd just come through. Her height was average; yet she'd still had to duck.

"Atmosphere," she said out loud to no one in particular. "Anything for pioneer effect. But then . . . why not?"

There was more pioneer effect right in front of her, for the door into the inn's only public washroom was just as small and would be sure to make a patron stoop. In fact, everything about the David Winkler House was small: the rooms, the halls, the doorways, the windows. But with clever restorations, the place seemed far more dainty than cramped. The David Winkler House had been built in the late eighteenth century by David Winkler — no surprise there — to accommodate his large family at a time when people were smaller than they are today. The present owners, the four innkeepers who had turned it into an extremely successful country dining room and inn, had been careful to preserve everything they could to make the place as authentic as possible.

From the moment Chris had left the graveled parking lot, which was quite carefully and deliberately separated from the building by a row of lilac bushes and a profusion of hollyhocks in full bloom, she had felt herself slide backward in time. The owners had done such a good job. From the squeaky gate in the stockade fence to the milk paint on the shutters to the weathered cedar shingles on the roof, the David Winkler House bespoke "authentic." And it bespoke "charm."

They had succeeded inside, too. Only someone who looked carefully for them would ever find electrical outlets or switches or wires. There was no evidence of a telephone anywhere, not even where the hostess greeted the guests. Even the washroom, where Chris now stood, was hidden away from the dining area. It couldn't be found without asking. Not easily, anyway.

Chris ducked and stepped inside, remembering why she'd come back here in the first place. There wasn't much room. Not only was it a unisex facility, it barely accommodated one person at a time. She pushed the door open right to the wall. It just cleared a sink styled in antique porcelain that stood on a thin pedestal in the corner ahead of her and to the left. On the wall opposite the door hung a framed mirror, surrounded by dried roses, dried fern, and Queen Anne's lace. To her right, the unavoidable stark modernity of the toilet was softened by an identical mirror on the wall above it, this one holding up a tangle of green foxtail. In a deliberate sequence, Chris flushed the toilet, turned each tap on, then off, and gently pushed the door closed.

"Not bad," she said, again out loud but to no one in particular. It was impossible to make a washroom look eighteenth century, certainly in what had been a pioneer home. But everything was designed for silence. The door did not squeak, and the plumbing was absolutely hushed. No modern noises to intrude on the atmosphere.

On the remaining wall hung the sampler that Kate Mistoe said she was nailing up when Menelaus Atko was shot. It was a delicately embroidered piece of work, set in a frame similar to that used for the mirrors. It didn't have the familiar proverb or Biblical quotation, however. This sampler held another oblique intrusion from the twentieth century. What it said, in very fine needlework, was:

> *O, Winkler patrons, please take heed,*
> *These things our septic does not need.*

A most unpoetic list of the jetsam of modern living followed: matches, cigarette butts, napkins, hairpins, aluminum foil. Chris counted nineteen items that Winkler patrons were not to throw into the toilet!

Kate Mistoe had been here in the washroom when Menelaus Atko was shot in the dining room earlier this morning. Or so she said. Her story was supported, though, by Sandy Sanchez. Sandy's account was that he was going past the washroom on his way to the propane tanks out back at the time the shots were fired. He and Kate had stared at each other for what seemed like forever, frozen in shock and fear. Then they wasted more precious time colliding with each other in the narrow hallway in their effort to get to the dining room where they found the body of Menelaus, bleeding but not breathing. Through the window, both swore they'd seen a blue car roar onto the road from the parking lot in a plume of gravel and exhaust.

That part of the story was verified in turn by Karl Schloss who had been driving up the road to the David Winkler

House from the opposite direction. He'd seen the blue car turn to the right in a skid at the intersection a short distance away, and then disappear. The dust from the gravel, according to Schloss, along with the exhaust, hung like a trail over the parking lot and down the road. Schloss had run into the dining room to find Sanchez and Mistoe clinging to each other, as far from the late Menelaus Atko as they could get.

All three, Mistoe, Sanchez, and Schloss, were now sitting in the kitchen waiting for Chris to finish her walkabout. To her, they were still prime suspects, in spite of the story of the blue car and the fact that their alibis all dovetailed so neatly.

Chris had questioned them separately an hour before. Schloss's story would be the easiest to check. He said he'd been in town at a service station getting the oil changed in his car. Normally that would make his alibi entirely solid, but there was a hitch. He had not come directly back to the Winkler House but had detoured via one of the farms where the inn bought fresh produce each day. When he saw that there was no one home there, he'd left and arrived back at the David Winkler House just in time to see the blue car speed away.

Sandy Sanchez, during his interview, had been exceptionally animated. As he spoke, his hands were constantly on the move in sweeping, dramatic gestures. The fittings on the propane tanks needed tightening, he'd said, making big round clockwise circles at Chris with his fist, as though he were holding a wrench. It was while he was on his way to do that, that he and Kate heard the shots.

Chris felt the man's animated style was natural; he probably talked that way all the time. In any case it would be easy enough to verify. So would his knowledge of propane systems. What bothered her most was that his story supported Kate Mistoe's, and it meant then that both were lying. So then what about Schloss? Was there a three-way conspiracy here at Winkler House?

One thing she had to do right away was talk to Atko's lawyer. The three prime suspects each owned ten percent of the inn. Atko held the rest. What she wanted to know was what kind of in-the-event-of-death clause there was in their partnership agreement. If Mistoe, Schloss, and Sanchez stood to gain substantially from their late partner's death, then . . .

► *Why does Chris Beadle believe that Kate Mistoe and Sandy Sanchez are lying? Why does she want to find out what Sandy Sanchez knows about propane systems? And how can she check out Karl Schloss's story?*

26

A Quiet Night with Danielle Steel?

▼

"Could be we've caught a bit of a break, Steve. According to the list of emergency telephone numbers at the kitchen phone, her regular physician lives two doors east of here. That'd be the odd-looking house with the cupola over the front portico? No lawn? Pushed right out to the street almost? There's a patrolman on the way over there right now. Maybe we can wrap this up without needing to do an autopsy. Almost for sure, no inquest, right?"

To anyone unacquainted with Steve Lanark, it would have looked like he was paying no attention whatever to his partner. Chantal Breton was used to these stone-faced responses, though. They had worked together for several years in a one-two ranking in the coroner's office. In fact it was widely expected that Chantal would take over as chief when Steve retired in three months, and widely held that she deserved to do so.

Chantal kept talking. "What we've got isn't all that dramatic, except maybe for the Jacuzzi." She wrinkled her nose and stared with dispassionate professional interest at the body lying in the now-cold water of the large bathtub.

"Woman in her late forties. Executive. Married and divorced twice. Lives alone. Sunday night she pours a scotch, fills the Jacuzzi, picks up the paperback she's got going, and gets into the tub. There's no marks or bruises, no signs of violence, no bumps on her head or back of her neck. She's even wearing her glasses.

"Tell you what." Chantal Breton looked around to be sure none of the police officers in the next room could hear. "I'll give you two to one the physician tells us she had a bad heart. Or very high BP.

"No, I'll go you one better! I'll give you *three* to one that if we have to do an autopsy, we don't find water in the lungs. Like, she died before going under the water. OK?"

Steve Lanark still behaved as if he did not even hear his partner. Instead he was hunched over a small ersatz marble slab on one side of the bathtub. It was about the size of an end table and, indeed, was designed to serve that purpose. At one corner of the slab, farthest from the tap end of the tub, a facecloth in a deep burgundy lay folded neatly with a bar of soap sitting on top. Neither had been used. At the diagonal corner, within easier reach, was a cocktail glass, its bottom still covered with the remains of a drink. Scotch, the two doctors had concluded earlier.

Steve appeared to be using the platform as a mirror to examine a shaving cut on his chin. The marble was ivory, with subtle streaks of gray and an occasional hint of ocher. Its surface was pristine, like the rest of the place, and gleamed in the high light.

"Really neat, this woman, wasn't she?" Chief Coroner Lanark spoke for the first time. He lifted his face from the side platform, but still didn't look at Chantal. "I mean, look at her robe there on the floor. She folded it before getting into the tub. How many people do you know do that?"

He got to his feet, arched his back, and then tapped first one foot on the floor then the other. "New shoes," he said. "I hate new shoes." He twisted his right foot like someone extinguishing a cigarette butt. "This whole place . . . Why don't you give one of those cops out front there a three to one that they can't find a toothpaste spatter on that mirror above the sink?"

"Or a dust bunny under her bed?" Chantal added. "Yeah, she's neat all right. Or else her cleaning lady comes in every day. I know what you mean about the shoes, by the way. You should try it from my end. Men have no idea at all what shoe designers do to women's feet. I mean, they expect that —"

"Help me lift the book out of the water." Steve interrupted what he knew would otherwise become an extended commentary on women's podiatric tribulations. "I think if we use that long-handled shoehorn over there, we won't have to get ourselves wet."

Silently Chantal went over to the back of the bathroom door and lifted the necessary implement off a hook and brought it over to the tub. It slid easily under the sodden paperback.

"Danielle Steel." Steve made no effort to control the distaste in his voice when he saw the cover. "Now tell me, is a woman like this going to read this kind of stuff? I mean, she's CEO of her firm, a big success. Appears to be a totally no-nonsense type. I mean, Danielle Steel?"

Chantal sighed with the patience of one long inured to male obtuseness. "Hey, it's her own private bathroom. It's the end of the day. She's got a Jacuzzi. She's having a drink. You want her to read Kierkegaard or something? Give me a break!"

Steve pursed his lips and nodded. "Yeah, I guess not," he agreed finally with a sigh, although his tone suggested he was not entirely convinced. Then he added somewhat grumpily, "And before you offer, I'm not taking any bets on whether we find more novels like this in the rest of the house. Whoever was in here after this woman died wouldn't be that stupid."

► *On what basis does Chief Coroner Steve Lanark conclude that someone was in the bathroom after the victim died?*

27

Right Over the Edge of Old Baldy

▼

Directly ahead about ten paces or so, a double white blaze on the trunk of a large oak told Pam Hall the trail turned sharply to the right. She paused for a moment, putting out her hand to lean on another oak. The edge of Old Baldy was just ahead but Pam chose to stop anyway to enjoy the moment. It was her favorite time of year, every hiker's favorite: early fall.

Absently shifting her backpack to a more comfortable spot, she let her eyes drift across the multihued canopy above her. Then she looked back down the trail toward Kimberley Rock, where she'd stopped for a drink of water about ten minutes ago. From Kimberley on there was almost no underbrush on the Bruce Trail. Just huge, old-growth forest enclosing a deep silence that even the birds respected, a silence that went right into the soul. It was like being in an empty cathedral in the late afternoon, one of those moments that all hikers know they share with cloistered monks and nuns.

Perhaps it was the silence. Certainly it was the deep peacefulness, the precious sense of the moment, that made the scream leave such a ragged tear in Pam's consciousness. It began as a moan. Even though it lasted only a second or two, this was the part that would linger more intensely than any other in her nightmares. At first it sounded almost like pleasure, not unlike the "aaahs" one frequently heard from people who first encountered the vista from the lip of Old Baldy. But there was no pleasure in this moan. It turned from an "aaah" into an "iieee" and then into a long "nooo" that faded out and away like oil running down a funnel. Someone had gone over the cliff.

Later, when Pam was explaining her suspicions about Hadley Withrop to the officer from the Park Service, she realized that the entire event had taken place only a minute or so ahead of her on the trail. It had been two years since she'd hiked this part of the escarpment and she wasn't aware she was quite so close to Old Baldy when it happened. That became another part of her nightmare. Had she not stopped at the double blaze to drink in the quiet, would Sheena Withrop still be alive? Or would she, Pam, have been pushed over the edge too?

Either way, she'd gotten there too late. When the scream first pierced Pam's senses and the logic of what was happening finally tumbled through, she found herself gripping the oak tree in panic with both hands, wasting precious seconds in the process of absorbing the shock. In her nightmare the next sequence always came back in slow motion: the bending over to pick up her walking stick and then inadvertently kicking it away so she had to bend again; the slosh of her water bottle working its way loose in her backpack as she ran up the trail, affecting her balance; the spiderweb that grabbed the bridge of her nose and pushed into both eyes as though it was trying to capture and hold her right there in the middle of the trail; the sight of a pair of turkey vultures circling high out over Beaver Valley, oblivious to the drama below them; and then, as she came up to the shaking Hadley Withrop at the edge of the cliff, the echo of Sheena's cry. An "aaah" and an "iieee" and a "nooo" all over again, in precisely that order.

She was sure she had heard an echo too. Positive. And her nightmare confirmed it. But it was also the part of her account that made the officer from the Park Service exchange quick glances with his partner. The doubt in their faces was plain.

"As I came up to Baldy," Pam told the officer, "he — Withrop — is standing there. Well, not quite standing. He's kinda bouncing around. You know, upset. Pacing.

"I think I really scared him. He obviously wasn't expecting anyone. Certainly didn't know I was on the trail. But he didn't say anything about that. He just said, 'She went over, she went over.' But not panicky, you know, not all cranked up like you'd expect. He talked to me like we'd just met on the trail. Casually, you know, as people do.

"'We just came up from Kimberley,' he said to me. 'Ate our lunch at the rock there. And we weren't here two minutes when . . .' Now that's when he started to cry. Went down to his knees and put his face in his hands, and started to shake. Really sounds like shock, doesn't it?

"But here's why I don't like his story, Officer," Pam added emphatically. "And I don't think you should like it either."

► *What is Pam Hall about to tell the officer from the Park Service that will explain why she doesn't accept Hadley Withrop's account of what happened?*

28

THE CASE OF QUEEN
ISABELLA'S GIFT

▼

Two monologues were fighting for attention in Geoff Dilley's brain. One was by Vicar Titteridge. He was talking about keys.

"Tourists would be entirely disappointed in these," he was saying as he took a pair of shiny brass keys from his pants pocket and inserted one into the padlock hanging from a hasp on the old church door.

"They much prefer this kind of thing, of course." He held up a worn leather thong in front of Geoff's face, dangling a huge, black iron key larger than his hand. "Interesting, what? Can't blame them, really, the tourists. A blacksmith made this quite some time before locksmiths and that sort of profession were ever heard of, you see."

Geoff wanted to point out that the Romans had padlocks, that the Chinese had used combination locks for centuries, and that in the Middle Ages locks were made that could count the number of times a key was inserted. But the vicar struck him as the type that was unaccustomed to contradiction.

"The key is almost two hundred years old, we think. Can't be proven, of course, but church records indicate the door here was replaced in the same year George IV became Prince Regent. You know, when his poor father went bonkers once and for all. At any rate, it's only logical to assume the key was made at the same time."

He rapped on the door firmly. "Solid oak this. From the New Forest. Very unusual that. Needed royal permission to cut the tree. Still, the door's a relative junior compared to the church itself: 1320 it was dedicated. Legend has it Edward II himself was here for the ceremony. Doesn't seem likely though, for it's sure that Queen Isabella was here. And you know about those two."

Geoff wanted to say that yes, he did know all about those two, but he didn't for the vicar had finally inserted the big key and turned it. The door opened easily and noiselessly, exposing the cool darkness inside. It occurred to Geoff that tourists would prefer some nice, authentic creaking, but he said nothing and waited in the doorway while the vicar stepped inside and turned on the lights.

"You'll have to come up to the altar," the vicar said. "The candelabra were up there."

"Candelabra" triggered the other monologue, the one Geoff Dilley had been trying to suppress. It came back again, though. Verbatim.

"*Candelabra!*" It was Chief Inspector Peddelley-Spens and he was shouting. "Bleedin' *candelabra?* We've got seven — count 'em, seven — homicide investigations going on at this precise moment. There's mad Irishmen bombin' the country to bleedin' bits. I've got a bunch o' bleedin fox-kissers chained t' the fence at Marlborough Hunt. The bleedin' prime minister o' bleedin Portugal is comin' this afternoon. And *you*! You want to investigate the theft of a bleedin' pair o' candelabra?" Peddelley-Spens stopped to take in a huge breath. "I suppose that next you'll want the weekend off, too, so you can join hands with those frog-kissers that want a bleedin' tunnel under the bleedin' M5?"

Suddenly, the Chief Inspector had softened to half volume. "One!" he said. "You can make one call!" And then to normal volume altogether. "Look, Geoffrey. I know how much you like bleedin' old things. But you're a good investigator. I need you here! Now you can trot off to — where is it? — St. Dunstan's-by-the-Water? But I want you back today before tea. Somebody's got to mind the crime rate while the rest of us are guardin' his Portuguese worship!"

Geoff's love of "bleedin' old things" — he had long ago despaired of instructing Peddelly-Spens in the use of "antiquarian" — made him more than anxious to visit St. Dunstan's-by-the-Water. He knew the ancient church but had never been in it. St. Dunstan's was a tiny but most unusual structure. A chapel really, rather than a church, but it was Norman and that made it special. Since it was built in the early fourteenth century, when Gothic architecture had wholly supplanted all other forms, St. Dunstan's lay claim to being the last piece of Norman architecture built in England.

In the hour it had taken him to drive there, Geoff came to realize he would never be able to make Peddelly-Spens appreciate just how valuable, how utterly priceless and irreplaceable the stolen candelabra really were.

"A gift of Queen Isabella," the vicar had said on the telephone. "You can still see her seal. Gold, of course. Each piece has some quite lovely stones, too."

Geoff knew that if the candelabra were not found right away, their fate would go one of two ways: they would either be fenced to a collector or, more likely, the stones would be pried out and the gold melted down. Either way, no one would ever see the ancient pieces again.

"Watch your step." The vicar's monologue returned just a shade too late to save Geoff from stumbling as they walked up the short aisle. "Original floors, you know. Even stone wears after six-and-a-half centuries."

Geoff had been following the vicar as slowly as possible so he could look around. He wanted to spend time in this church. It was Norman, all right. Thick walls, round arches, windows that looked more like arrow slits.

"Right there. Above the altar. They stood on those two pedestals."

Geoff stared at the altar.

"No, no. Higher. Up there." The vicar directed Geoffrey's gaze to a point well above the altar where two small stone platforms jutted out from the columns leading from the ends of the altar to the roof.

"I assume . . ." the vicar was still talking. Other than introducing himself, Geoffrey had yet to say a word. "I assume he, or she — maybe even *they*. There were several dozen strangers here last night. Isn't it curious how we automatically believe it is males who commit crime? — I assume the perpetrator, or perpetrators, attended Evensong last night and then hid in the church until it was empty. The candelabra were definitely here, for they were lit. Everyone saw them. They're only lit for Evensong. Too much of a bother, even with a step stool and extended candlelighters. And I assume that since we lock the main door on the outside as you saw, that he or she or they went out here."

The vicar led Geoff to a door behind the altar. "It's the only other way in or out," he said. "A concession to the twentieth century. Fire regulations and all that, you see."

He leaned against the crash bar, covering the little red-and-silver sign that said "Emergency Exit Only" with his bottom, and opened the door. Geoff followed him outside and turned to watch the door close and lock automatically.

"When I'm alone, I normally enter this way." The vicar produced the pair of brass keys again and opened the door. "Less fuss. Did so this morning."

Geoff followed the vicar back inside.

"Really don't know what made me look up. At any rate they were gone, and straight away I rushed back out and telephoned you."

For the first time, Geoffrey opened his mouth and was actually going to speak, but the vicar anticipated his question and beat him to it. "You're going to ask me about the verger, aren't you? Well, we don't have one at St. Dunstan's. Poor old Albert died over a year ago, and we never arranged for a replacement. This is only a chapel, really. A Sunday morning service and then Evensong, so there's no need. One of the parishioners comes every second Tuesday. I let her in and we clean together."

Geoff took a breath and got out "How . . ." before the vicar said, "There were between forty and fifty last night. About fifteen regulars. No, no. This way."

Geoff had turned to go out behind the altar.

"So we can turn the lights out and double lock the main door again. Pity we have to do that. House of God and all that, but then I certainly don't have to tell you about it. The crime rate, I mean."

The vicar paused to straighten a hymn book, and Geoffrey blurted, "No, Vicar. I know all about it." The voice of Peddelley-Spens rumbled like distant thunder in the back of his mind. "But it's even worse when a man of the cloth adds to it. The crime rate, I mean."

► *Why has Geoff Dilley concluded that Vicar Titteridge has stolen the pair of candelabra?*

29

MURDER AT
249 HANOVER STREET

▼

As she pulled over to the curb, Janet Dexel cocked her head a little closer to the portable radio on the seat beside her.

"The wettest first day of October since records were started in 1826," the announcer was saying, "and the outlook for the next several days is more of the same."

Janet snapped off the radio and peered almost gloomily across the sidewalk at 249 Hanover Street. "A perfectly miserable day," she said out loud to herself, "and now a perfectly miserable night and a perfectly miserable place over there to go with it all."

Certainly, 249 Hanover Street was not inviting. Although the brick pillars supporting the heavy gates, together with the wrought iron fence, would never keep out any determined intruder, they said "You Are Not Welcome" in a most effective way. If the message failed here, at the edge of the property, then the double doors under the dimly lit portico at the house itself took a second stab at it, for their design repeated the warning that visitors to 249 Hanover Street would not be pleasantly received.

Janet groaned as she forced herself out of the car into the pouring rain. She drew her heavy rain cloak tight around her shoulders and stared at the big house for a few seconds before walking back to an empty squad car parked at the curb behind her. She leaned in and switched off the flashing red lights, then made a note of the car's number before turning to walk quickly through the open gates. Staff Sergeant Janet Dexel hated fuss. She especially disliked police operations that attracted attention unnecessarily. Someone in her unit was going to get a dressing down as soon as she had the opportunity, and at the moment, the odds favored tonight.

Rain began to fall even harder so she broke into a run for the last few steps up to the double doors. Once inside, the sight of Chesley Barron-Ripple, or rather, what had been Chesley Barron-Ripple, quickly took her mind off the bad weather and the fool who had left the lights flashing. Two of her officers stood over the body. Neither was enjoying the assignment very much. One of them held a handkerchief over her nose.

Chesley Barron-Ripple was attracting the kind of attention that would have embarrassed him beyond measure had he been alive. An assistant from the medical examiner's office was snapping picture after picture of him where he lay on a priceless, silk-on-silk handwoven rug. Behind the police officers, a pair of ambulance attendants, looking far more at ease than anyone else at the scene, were holding a body bag like a pair of Boy Scouts about to fold the flag at the end of the ceremony.

One of the policemen, the younger one, almost stood at attention as he addressed his boss. "The lab people have all gone, Sergeant," he said. "Except for him." The policeman nodded at the photographer. "And he's almost finished — *Aren't you?*"

It was clear to Janet that everyone wanted to get this part of the investigation over and done with.

"We're waiting for you to give us the clear." It was the other officer. She was speaking through her handkerchief. "Detective Andrew is in the next room with the three . . . uh . . . I guess they're suspects, aren't they?"

"Oh? Suspects?" Another thing that bothered Janet was having her officers jump to conclusions. Especially if there were media people nearby. One positive outcome of the heavy rain, however, was that the situation was free of the press, at least so far.

"Well, I mean . . . I don't know if they're suspects. They're . . . they're . . . they've been *detained* by Detective Andrew."

The officer appeared relieved that she'd found the right word.

"There are three people," she continued with more confidence now. "There's the part-time handyman. And Barron-Ripple's daughter, and . . . and . . ." Her discomfort had returned. "And the *butler*, Sergeant Dexel."

Before Janet could reply, the younger policeman spoke again. "He said he was the butler, Sergeant, but I think he's really a kind of valet or personal servant. Anyway, he's got an alibi. He went to his sister's in Kennebunkport on the 30th. Been there for two days. Actually, all three have got alibis like that."

"I see," Janet Dexel said, searching her coat pockets for a tissue to pat the droplet of rain on her eyelash.

"Yeah, the daughter, Sergeant Dexel," the policewoman was still talking through her handkerchief. "She's . . . well . . . her alibi's pretty solid. She's been drying out in a clinic for the past month. Got back this morning. When she got home here she saw the butler . . . uh . . . valet, I guess, standing on the portico. Seems neither of them had a key so they sent for the handyman. He lives over in Lower Sackville.

"And what's *his* cover?" Janet wanted to know.

"Sounds reasonable enough," was the answer. "He comes once a week unless there's something special to do. Tomorrow's his day, and he missed last week. Says his wife and two neighbors can back it up."

"I see." Janet nodded at the body and then at the two ambulance attendants who still held the body bag stretched out. "I guess you can move him out of here now." To the police officers she said, "You two tell Andrew to advise that butler or valet or whatever he calls himself of his rights and then bring him downtown. I'll meet him there. Shouldn't be too hard to break up his story. You were right about 'suspect.' Just don't say it. Leave that kind of talk for the lawyers."

► *What is Janet Dexel's reason for suspecting the butler rather than the daughter or handyman?*

30

WAITING OUT
THE RAIN

▼

Michelle Link sat in one of the two window booths at Kline's Soda Shoppe with Julie Varughese and two of their classmates from Memorial Junior School. All four stared gloomily at the rain pelting down on the street outside. They had headed straight for Kline's right after school, beating the crowd so they could get their favorite booth. It was a perfect location. In the corner at the window, the booth gave them a sweeping view of everybody in the little restaurant — more important, they could see who came in *with* whom and not be too obvious about it. As well, if the patrons failed to stir up any interest, they could usually find something diverting out on the street.

Not today, though. Except for two older ladies who had come in for tea, Kline's was unusually empty. So was the street. The rain had begun to fall the instant they arrived, hard enough to discourage any of the regulars from Memorial Junior and, except for two pedestrians who had taken shelter in the doorway of Vex's Pharmacy across the way, hard enough to pretty much empty the street, too. Now, two Cherry Cokes apiece later, and having exhausted the day's school stories, the four friends were bored and quite ready to leave, but the rain was not yet prepared to let them.

The only distraction, and the only person who seemed to be enjoying the weather, was a little boy standing in the gutter just off the sidewalk a few feet away from Michelle. He couldn't be more than three, Michelle calculated, watching him stand there in the water that sluiced down the gutter around his bright blue rubber boots, splashing up against and almost over the toes where someone — an older sister, Michelle speculated — had painted a large "L" on top of one and an "R" on the other with pink fingernail polish.

Through Kline's screened door, Michelle could hear the boy's squeal of delight as a candy-bar wrapper floated up to the toes, then made a complete circle and carried on between the boots. She followed the progress of the wrapper for a few feet and for the first time noticed the woman on the edge of the sidewalk. Must be the kid's mother, her speculation continued.

The woman was not watching her son — if it really was her son. She was standing under the awning at Whippany Appliances next door, listening transfixed to the radio bulletin booming from the store. Whippany Appliances was advertising Motorola, their new franchise brand, and a big cabinet model standing just inside the door put the news out onto the street.

Michelle could hear it from the restaurant:

". . . from General Eisenhower's headquarters in England a confirmation that five divisions are involved: two American, two British, one Canadian. Early reports indicate that German troops have fallen back from the beaches at all five landing areas. Pockets of resistance are still strong, however, at Omaha Beach.

"The Columbia Broadcasting System's news service has also learned that . . ."

For the past two days the radio news had talked of nothing but the landings at Normandy, the biggest invasion, it was being described, in the history of warfare. Michelle watched the woman stare vaguely into the appliance store. She had not once turned around to look at her little boy. He had his rain hat off now and was filling it with water.

"Michelle! Earth to Michelle! Hey, get with it! The rain has stopped! Remember? The wet stuff? Let's go while we can!" Julie finally reached across the table and shook her friend's arm.

"I wonder if her husband's a soldier?" Michelle said, without looking at Julie. "The little boy's father. I'll bet he is."

"What *are* you talking about?" Julie shook Michelle's arm one more time. "C'mon! The rain's let up. We've got to leave now or we'll have to order another Cherry Coke. Either that or rent the booth."

Michelle and Julie said goodbye to their friends at the doorway to Kline's and headed up the street. For a few seconds, they, too, paused at Whippany Appliances and listened to the radio talk about Normandy. The woman and the little boy were gone. Somehow they had disappeared as the girls were getting out of the booth. The street began to fill with activity again, almost as if it had been waiting, pent up and hidden under shelter until the weather improved.

The two pedestrians from Vex's Pharmacy had crossed the street and were moving on ahead of the girls. Farther up they could see Mr. Lum at Lum's Groceteria pushing carts of fruit and vegetables back onto the sidewalk. Next to the appliance store two men got out of a truck belonging to Bitnik's

Delivery Service and began to wrestle a soaking wet tarpaulin off a stack of cardboard boxes. Cars began to move up the street more quickly now, as though relieved by the prospect of drier progress.

Two minutes later, at the corner of Vine Street, Julie said goodbye, peeling off down Vine, leaving Michelle to continue on two more blocks to her home on Sanders Avenue. Michelle didn't expect to speak to Julie again until school the next day. For one thing, there was too much homework. More important, her parents had made one of those suggestions that parents tend to make about too much use of the phone on school nights.

The telephone rang anyway, about an hour after dinner, and it was Julie.

"Did you *hear* what happened? At Kline's?"

Michelle wanted to point out that obviously she had not, or why would Julie be calling, but she didn't get a chance.

"There was an accident! You know that truck? Bitnik's truck?" Julie was very wound up.

"It was right there when we passed. Remember? Those two guys unloading . . . uh . . . whatever it was? Anyway, *it rolled right into Kline's!* Right through the *window!* My dad says the brakes, no, no, the *emergency* brake probably failed."

"Julie . . ."

"I mean, right where we were sitting!"

"Julie . . ."

"Can you imagine? Like . . . if it hadn't stopped raining? We'd have been sitting right there! We could have been killed! Or really injured or something!"

"Not just us, Julie. But listen . . ."

"Don't tell your parents we were sitting right there in the window booth. I mean, I didn't tell *my* parents. You know what it's like. They'll get all worried and then they'll start thinking Kline's is dangerous and then . . . well . . . anyway. You know what parents are like. But isn't it *exciting*?

"Julie!"

There was a pause followed by a soft and very tentative "What?"

"Julie, that was no accident."

► *Why is Michelle Link sure that what Julie Varughese has described was not an accident?*

31

THE BODY ON
BLANCHARD BEACH

▼

Like the others sitting on the side facing the window, Sue Cremer pulled her chair closer to the table as soon as K.D. Lapp came in. Everyone did it automatically and almost at the same time, a habit they'd developed because K.D. always whipped his crutches forward one after the other in a wide half-circle, and he needed extra room to get by.

As her boss settled in at the head of the long table, it occurred to Sue that she might have lost her carefully planned advantage in the pull forward. This afternoon's meeting was about the body found on Blanchard Beach earlier in the day. There would be slides projected at the wall across from K.D. Lapp, slides of the site and — the reason Sue Cremer had got her usual early seat — slides of the murdered body.

For two years as director of Information Services in the office of the county coroner, she had successfully avoided ever looking at a dead body, either the real thing or even a picture. It was a secret she'd kept from her colleagues all this time by doing things like sitting third chair from the end on Chief Coroner Lapp's right. That strategy ensured she would always have the obsessive Doctor Reuven Shallmar immediately beside her, blocking her view of the screen. Shallmar was a brilliant pathologist whose forensic skills were almost as legendary as the tantrums he threw whenever his notions of order and sequence were disturbed. One of those notions was that he had the right, always and absolutely without exception, to sit in the same place at every staff meeting. No one opposed him.

The man's wishes and his peculiar behavior made no difference whatever to Sue. What mattered to her was Shallmar's abnormally large head, made even larger by a sunburst of crinkly red hair. She had learned through practice that by sitting just so, she could appear to be gazing intently at the screen when in fact her line of sight was entirely obscured by the pathologist's mighty skull.

When the call came down for today's meeting she had, as usual, positioned herself with time to spare, for this was going to be a bad one. In the past six months two bodies had been found on Blanchard Beach, at different times but less than a kilometer apart. Both had been adult females and both had been mutilated after death. Whoever was responsible was a very sick person. The tabloid press was already ranting about a serial killer and the more responsible media was on the brink of joining the chorus. This morning's discovery of a third body was sure to tip them over the edge. That's why, in every office around the city that was even remotely connected to law enforcement, there had been meetings like this going on all day.

Chief Coroner Lapp rapped his knuckles for attention.

"All right, people. Let's get on task here. I'm leaving for

the police commissioner's office in thirty minutes and I want to be able to take something with me from this meeting. Now the slides we have here are — Ah! Dexter. Thank you for coming."

The door had opened after a single knock. A short black man moved along the wall to an extra chair between Lapp and the window. He wore jeans and a faded T-shirt that loudly proclaimed "No Sweat, Mon!" over an oasis of sand and waving palms.

Lapp introduced him. "I'm not sure all of you know Dexter Treble. These are his photographs we're about to look at and I've asked him to narrate." He lowered his voice slightly. "Can we get going on this right away, Dexter? I'm due at the commissioner's task force and . . ." He let his sentence drift away while Dexter Treble beamed a smile in return.

Dexter acknowledged Lapp's request: "Of course!" Contrary to the initial impression his appearance may have created with some at the table, Dexter was efficient, articulate, and possessed of a crisp British accent.

"Of course," he repeated, and picked up the remote control, turning on the slide projector in the same fluid motion. "It would be helpful if someone could dim the, ah, thank you.

"The first photograph here," Dexter clicked a slide into position on the carousel "is of the pertinent section of the area known as Blanchard Beach. It's not my work. This is from the county files. It was taken by the pollution control group about a year ago. No particular significance to our work here other than I thought it would be germane for you to be reminded of what Blanchard Beach looks like when it's not famous, or rather, infamous."

Sue edged forward slightly to see around Reuven Shallmar's bobbing mane. The photograph was a safe one and she had been in the beach area only once before. Blanchard was a lonely stretch about ten minutes' drive from the edge of the city. The beach itself, between the sand dunes and the water, was flat and sandy, but swimming was banned because of a fierce undertow. It was a lonely place most of the time. Even teenagers chose other spots to drag race and carry on. An ideal place to dump things. Sue was leaning forward intently when Dexter Treble clicked in the next slide without warning. Her stomach lurched but then calmed. The shot was innocuous enough. It was a body wrapped in something brown.

"This is taken from a dune looking down on the site. One of mine." Dexter carried on smoothly. "According to the couple that discovered the body, this is exactly what they saw when they came upon it. As you can see, there is the body, then a single set of tire tracks. A remarkably clean site actually. No footprints, unfortunately, but the tread marks from the tires are quite clear. The police lab is working on those right now."

Dexter Treble popped ahead to a close-up of the tire treads in the sand. They were a perfect set. Sue found herself leaning forward just a bit more as Dexter went back to the previous slide.

"Notice the symmetry too. The investigating officer believes that the vehicle was reversed in and driven out after disposing of the cargo. The body itself was wrapped in that beige tarpaulin just as you see. That's the right hand of the victim protruding ever so slightly. Without the hand it would have been difficult to distinguish the body from other flotsam on the beach, especially from a distance. Now, if there were any doubt about murder, this next slide . . ."

Just in time, Sue slid back to safety behind Doctor Shallmar as Dexter clicked in the slide she'd been dreading, but in that second the door opened without a warning knock.

It was one of the young whitecoats from the morgue down-stairs. He was excited.

"Cadaver's here, Doctor Lapp."

Reuven Shallmar jumped to his feet. "What I've been waiting for!" He turned to the door, then stopped heron-like on one leg and looked back to K.D. Lapp. "Kirk?"

K.D. Lapp waved him on. "Yes, by all means. Call me at the commissioner's office in one hour, no matter what."

Shallmar was released into flight before Lapp even finished speaking. Almost without warning, Sue Cremer's protective barrier had disappeared!

Later that evening she was unable to explain, even to herself, how she'd carried it off, but the instant Doctor Shallmar slammed the door she turned away from the screen to face her boss.

"Doctor Lapp," she said calmly, "could we return to the previous slide, please?"

He looked at her with mild curiosity. Sue almost never spoke at these meetings. Lapp nodded to Dexter, who imme-diately returned to the close-up of the tire tracks.

"No, sorry. The one before that," Sue insisted.

Dexter accommodated. By now everyone was staring at Sue instead of the screen. More dramatically than was her style, she swept her arm along the table and then pointed at the screen.

"Do you know, Dr. Lapp," she began to wave her finger at the screen in remonstrating fashion, "do you know whether the search for a vehicle has concentrated on a van, by any chance?"

K.D. Lapp peered at Sue and then looked back at the screen.

"By Jove," he said. Then louder. "By Jove!" He grabbed at his crutches. "I don't believe so, not to my knowledge! I don't believe so! By Jove!"

He caught his crutches on the edge of his chair and they clattered to the floor. "Drat!" he shouted at them.

Sue rose to her feet quickly. "I'll go do the telephoning, sir. You're needed here anyway."

Without waiting for an answer, Sue Cremer got to her feet and exited the room, being careful not to look at the screen just in case Dexter Treble decided to move ahead before she was ready.

▸ *Sue Cremer has successfully extricated herself from the meeting and at the same time provided what may be a valuable clue. Why does she believe the body was brought to Blanchard Beach in a van?*

32

The Case of the Missing Child

▼

The tension between the couple was like static electricity, ready to crackle at the first sign of movement. But from where Audrey Greenwood stood in the doorway, it didn't appear there was going to be any movement unless she initiated it. Downstairs, when she'd first come in, the couple had taken great care to avoid any contact with each other, like a pair of magnets carrying the same charge. Now it continued in the bedroom.

The father stood with his back to one of the windows, arms folded tightly across his chest, the old-fashioned venetian blinds framing his rigid vertical stance. Audrey felt that this corner room was ideal for the tableau inside, for the mother stood equally erect at the window on the south wall. She, however, held her arms akimbo and was staring resolutely out the window into the apartments across the street.

As it turned out, the tension had an ultimate benefit in the case, for its force made Audrey pause longer in the doorway than she otherwise might have. Normally, in cases like this, when she was first to arrive, she would assert herself quickly so that no matter which way headquarters decided to play it, the victims involved would see her as the principal investigator. Audrey worked out of Juvenile Branch, a more effective group, in her opinion, than the stumblebums from Felonious Crimes, one of whom would arrive shortly. On the surface, the issue was either a kidnapping with, quite possibly, murder involved, or a simple runaway.

The room where the two parents stood braced for combat was a child's bedroom in metamorphosis from nursery to little-girl sanctuary. There was a diaper-changing table along the wall the father was facing, but, covered in Barbie Doll paraphernalia, it seemed to have outgrown its original purpose. The bed on the fourth wall had only recently been a crib, but the sides were gone now. Only the wallpaper, a rigorously gender-balanced mix of pink and blue cherubs, obviously chosen before the child's birth, had survived the change so far.

The crayon marks on the wallpaper were the first indication to Audrey that there might be something different about this child. There were just too many of them. They were too random, too thick. Then there was the tiny shelf near the ceiling. Way too high and out of reach to be normally functional, it was clearly purpose-built. An empty pharmacy bottle suggested what it had once been used for. Other things begged to be explained too, especially the nails in the window frames. Like the blinds, the windows were old, this being one of three late-Depression-era buildings holding out against a growing forest of new high-rise apartments. But the windows were nailed shut. Behind the father, Audrey could easily see the nails protruding from both frames.

"Lexie has a behavior disorder." Was the mother reading her mind? The voice continued through lips that barely moved. "The doctors don't know what it is. We've — No! *I've* taken her to, oh God, it seems like a hundred of them. She's got drugs, but they don't work. Sometimes I think they make her worse. She's a head-banger, she runs, she screams . . . I, oh God . . ."

For the first time, the mother's defenses seemed to weaken. Her shoulders drooped and brought her head down.

Out of experience, Audrey resisted any feelings of sympathy as she turned to the father. "This morning, when you first noticed she was missing . . ."

"It's happened a couple of times," he sighed. "Once we found her under the laundry tub, the other time in a broom closet. That's why we didn't call you right away. We searched the house first. When we couldn't find her —"

"Your call was logged at 7:44 AM," Audrey interrupted him. "When did you see her bed was empty?"

This time the woman spoke up. "My clock radio's set for 7:20. See, sometimes she sleeps in. It's rare but it happens, so just in case . . . She's got to have medication before eight or the day's pure hell. Anyway, Buzz got up when the radio went off, and he . . . well, when he couldn't find her he woke me up and we called 9-1-1."

Audrey nodded. "When did you last see her, then?"

"When she was put to bed last night," the father answered. "Just after eight. We both did it."

"The second time you've helped this month!" Her rigid stance had returned. "Don't tell me this is a trend!"

Audrey ignored the sarcasm and put her next question

before the father could lay out the response she saw was coming. "Didn't either of you, er, before you went to bed yourselves . . ."

"Go in to check? Tuck her in?" The mother's posture had stiffened even more. "Lexie is not very tuckable. Once she's asleep, you don't take a chance on waking her up. Sometimes her day starts at midnight. Anything can set her off — light, unfamiliar noise, even the wrong cooking smell." She slumped noticeably. "Besides, I fell asleep in front of the TV." The slump got lower and her voice became a pleading whisper. "Look. You don't know how exhausting it is to have a child like Lexie. It never stops! I . . . I just fell asleep."

By now she could barely be heard. Audrey could see tears.

"That's right." It was the father. "I was out last night. My poker night. Once a month. It's the only night I ever have for myself. I got back — oh, it had to be about 1:30 — and she, er, Jean, she was asleep in the living room. The TV was on, so I turned it off and covered her with a blanket.

"Before you ask — No, I didn't go in to Lexie's room either. You soon learn around here that when it's quiet you leave well enough alone."

The doorbell rang, making all of them jump. Audrey's partner had arrived.

"What have you touched in here this morning?" Audrey asked hastily. "You know, what have —"

"When I came in with you just now," the mother interrupted, "that's the first time since last night when I — oh goodness — when we put her to bed."

"And you, sir?" Audrey looked at the father.

"Just opened the door," he said. "Came in a few steps, I guess. Looked under the bed, of course." He paused. "Well, you can see the covers are peeled right down. It was obvious Lexie wasn't in the bed."

Audrey nodded and stepped back down the hall a bit. "Up here!" she called. "But we're coming down." She motioned to the mother and father to follow her and then called downstairs again. "This one is yours!"

▶ *Audrey Greenwood has decided that this is not a juvenile crime, such as a runaway or a missing child, but a felony. What has led her to that decision?*

33

THE CASE OF THE
ATTEMPTED SUICIDE

▼

The day, quite simply, had turned into a string of surprises
for Doug Nicholson. In the first place, police captains didn't
take cases, not on Doug's force anyway. They stayed in the
office to oversee things, to administer, to make sure subordi-
nates ran their cases properly. Yet here he was in the elegant
library of Berenice Devone, sitting in an uncomfortable chair,
waiting for tea — and the opportunity to question the lady.

This was only the first surprise, and it was easy to explain.
Doug had to do this investigation himself because his department was understaffed, what with the crime rate and all
the time-off requests over the Christmas holiday. Besides, the
case was only a wrap-up, a routine report to cover an
attempted suicide: Mrs. Devone's husband, Owen, had shot
himself three days before and was still in critical condition
in hospital.

Doug's second surprise was running into Owen Devone's secretary. Ms. Jasmine Peak was next on the list of those to be questioned. While he was pressing the button to ring the door chimes at the Devone mansion, she had driven up the circular drive and parked behind him. A surprise — but then she worked for the Devones. Why shouldn't she be there?

Their exchange of introductions had been awkward, however. Not his fault, Doug felt. He had identified himself out of a combination of courtesy and old police habit, but Mrs. Peak was extraordinarily self-conscious and barely mumbled her name. That had been a third surprise: Owen Devone's firm specialized in worldwide tea and coffee contracts, and one would have expected a secretary who spent part of her day on transoceanic phone calls and another part dealing in international trade to exhibit more confidence. So, another surprise — and it wasn't over yet.

Doug had expected a maid or a butler or some domestic to answer the door. When Berenice Devone herself opened it, he was taken aback.

"You must be Captain Nicholson." Berenice Devone was the last word in graciousness, and apparently not the least bit distressed. "Do come in . . . and you, Miss? . . . oh . . . you must be Miss Peak! I saw you at the hospital, didn't I? That was such an awful time."

Doug had then learned, on the way to the library, that Jasmine Peak had been an employee of the firm for only two weeks when the shooting incident occurred. He had also learned that there were no servants. This latter surprise explained why Berenice Devone had answered the door herself and then left them to make tea. But no servants at all? In a house like this? It just didn't figure.

The answer came without his asking, from the remarkably gracious — and candid — Mrs. Devone.

"I suppose you are aware of Owen's difficulties of late,"

she said as she came through the French doors with a simple but beautiful Limoges tea service. Her return with the refreshments was a relief to Doug. Jasmine Peak was entirely incapable of small talk. He didn't want to question her here, and the chit-chat about Christmas festivities — the only logical topic — seemed hollow in light of Owen Devone's recent behavior.

"He lost a great deal in Sri Lanka," Berenice Devone said as she poured milk, then tea, into the cup in front of Jasmine Peak. She could talk and serve simultaneously, Doug noted, and do both with polished accomplishment. But there was no surprise in that.

"'Bet on the wrong side.' That's how he put it. You know about the political troubles there. All but one of the plantations with which Owen had contracts simply failed to produce any tea at all." She lifted the lid of the teapot and peered inside professionally.

"Then the frosts in Colombia turned the coffee market into a shambles. Milk or lemon, Captain? Do you know there has never been a frost of that magnitude in Colombia?"

"Uh . . . milk, please." Doug was almost reluctant to interrupt.

"Then with all the pressure for product from his clients . . . I guess poor Owen just caved in."

The monologue stopped for just a moment.

"Of all times . . . on Christmas Eve!" she sighed heavily, then immediately offered round a plate of delicate unsugared wafers.

"Mrs. Devone, I'm going to have to look at the room where he . . ." Doug had wondered how he was going to bring this up but — another surprise — it seemed so easy. Mrs. Devone's composure had given him courage.

"Of course, Captain. It's a guest bathroom on the second floor. I'll take you there."

The intrusive ring of the telephone made all three of them jump. For the first time, Berenice Devone's control slipped. When she set her teacup down her hand shook, and beneath the ever so correctly applied makeup, her face had paled.

"It's the hospital, I know it's the hospital."

"Let me answer it." Doug rose from his chair and picked up the antique-style receiver. It was his office.

"For me," he whispered to Berenice Devone, tapping his chest with his forefinger, and then he turned to the mouthpiece. "No, I'll be here just a bit longer than I thought. There's been one surprise too many."

► *What has made Doug Nicholson suspicious?*

34

The Mission in the Clearing

▼

They had left the Land Rover in the bush and come in the last mile or so on foot. That had been the intent in any case, but because of the condition of the road they really had no choice. Curiously, instead of improving as they got closer to the little mission, the road had become worse, so that there was no question of proceeding without headlamps on. The moonless night was just too dark and the growth too thick. Even on foot they'd had trouble getting through quietly, but they'd made it without being discovered — or so they thought — and now the four of them were kneeling in the long grass at the edge of the clearing.

The squad was down to four, because the two Kikuyu "Home Guard" who normally rode on the roof of the Rover had disappeared shortly after the message came in on the wireless. Just melted away in the darkness. WO/I Ron

Forrester had experienced this once before in an almost identical situation, and he wasn't really surprised. At bottom, he didn't blame them. These auxiliaries were called "government loyalists," but Ron knew that if their fellow Kikuyu in the Mau Mau ever caught them, they'd suffer a lot longer and a lot harder than the white soldiers in his squad.

What truly irritated Ron, however, and frightened him, too, was the loss of the wireless. Its battery pack, actually, for that was what the operator, Lance Corporal Haight-Windsor, had dropped under the rear wheel. The squad could do without Haight-Windsor. He was back with the Rover, nursing his broken arm, still drunk in all likelihood. Ron swore that when they got back to base, Haight-Windsor was going to be busted yet again, this time to private, but only after a nice long dryout in the stockade.

A message had come in two hours ago, the product of one of those radio wave flukes that amaze everyone and surprise no one. It was a call for help originating from St. Ignatius-in-the-Forest Mission, probably from one of the still smoldering huts in front of them. It had been picked up by a ham operator a continent away in Somerset. He managed to get the local police to believe him, and then, via a series of telephone calls, the message had been relayed to Nairobi and thence to Ron's base back in Nyeri. Major Bowman himself had called from there.

His booming voice over a burst of static had jerked them all awake. Good thing, too, for the last watch of the night was Haight-Windsor's and that was when he'd gotten drunk. It was during loadup that he dropped the battery pack.

The order was simple: "Divert from the patrol and proceed with all possible haste to St. Ignatius-in-the-Forest Mission. Use extreme caution. Under attack by Mau Mau terrorists."

An improbable name, St. Ignatius-in-the-Forest, but the

mission was run by an equally improbable group of Jesuits from England. Against all advice they had refused to close it when the Mau Mau uprising had begun in earnest. On the contrary, the two fathers who ran the place had only just been relieved by two young seminary graduates fresh from Liverpool. Ron had never met them; he didn't even know their names. But he'd heard they were even more adamant than their predecessors about keeping the mission open. Now it seemed they were paying a price for their determination.

From where he knelt in the long grass, the light from the slowly rising sun told Ron that whatever had happened here, it was over, and the Mau Mau attackers were gone. Along with everyone else, it seemed. Or maybe they'd gotten out like the two Kikuyu auxiliaries. All but one of the buildings, the tiny schoolhouse, had been burned, destroyed. There was no sign of life anywhere, not even bodies. If there was anyone here, he (or she — Ron couldn't remember whether the nuns had finally left or not) would have to be in the schoolhouse.

Several yards to Ron's left, PFC Willie Throckton shifted slightly to avoid a cramp. He looked over at Ron with eyebrows raised, and swung the barrel of his Lee Enfield Mark IV toward the schoolhouse. Ron signaled back "just hold on," then crawled to his right, where the two others, Barrow and Highland, were concealed behind the mission's upturned GMC pickup. From here, Ron reconnoitered once more, using the new perspective to confirm his strategy.

Without taking his eyes off the school, he spoke to Barrow. "S.O.P. I'm putting a grenade over there for diversion. Then Throckton's going in first. We cover. He shelters on the shadow side. When he's in, you go to the other side."

Barrow just nodded. They were an experienced team and had done this before. Even Haight-Windsor, like the rest of them, had done two tours in Korea only a few years before.

Ron leaned back to be sure Highland was listening. He was.

"You're staying," he said to Highland. "I'm pretty sure the place is empty. If there's no return fire, I'm going straight in the door."

Highland simply nodded and ran his index finger along the grenades in his belt.

No more than ten seconds passed between the time Warrant Officer I Ron Forrester threw the grenade and when he burst through the door of the schoolhouse. There had been no return fire.

Ron stood in the schoolhouse for a few seconds more, then called, "Looks clear! I'm okay! Stay alert!"

It was not Mau Mau style to stick around after an attack, but he was taking no chances.

The shambles in the schoolhouse was to be expected. Quickly Ron took in the scene. Benches and tables were piled in disarray along both side walls. With their *pangas* the attackers had chopped up the school's paltry few books and scattered them around. A huge gouge had been cut out of the already dilapidated chalkboard. Particular care had been taken with the crucifix. It was barely recognizable. What really held Ron's attention, though, was the two dead priests in the center of the room.

Strangely, there was no evidence of torture, but that might have been because the squad's approach had been heard or seen, after all. Both men lay facedown in a pool of their own blood. Their arms had been cut from elbow to wrist, ritually, and it appeared they had bled to death. The right leg of one priest was bound at the ankle to the left leg of his partner with a leather thong that must also have had ritual significance, for small animal bones dangled from it at precise intervals. Both men still wore their shoes and Ron couldn't help reflecting on the improbable contrast of the mystical thong and the sturdy, sensible black Oxfords. One was scuffed from top to bottom at the back of the heel, the other — in fact both shoes belonging to the other priest — sparkled with a fresh buffing. It almost seemed as if he, like his attackers, had done some ritual preparation, for his cassock, too, was clean and new, and his hair neatly combed, unlike the priest on the left, whose appearance was unkempt, disheveled.

Both men, however, lay in the same position on the floor, and when he saw the nails, Ron suddenly knew what the attackers had had in mind. He looked again at the chopped-up crucifix and shuddered. It was well the Mau Mau had heard the squad coming.

Taking a few steps, he picked up one of the nails, then, for the first time, noticed the key ring lying under the remains of a bench near the wall. With his foot he dragged it out and picked it up. It had an ignition key. That he recognized. Another key — he had no idea what it was for. There were two brass disks. Both said D.M. Vincent, S.J., on one side. On the opposite, one said, A+, and the other said, Dipth. W.C. Typhoid 12/07/54.

He put the ring in his shirt pocket, then looked around cursorily for more things like it. When he saw nothing, he reluctantly bent over the bodies and began to pat their pockets for belongings. Nothing. A white band on the wrist of one of them said there had once been a wristwatch there, but it was gone.

Ron rocked back on his heels for a minute, wrapping his arms around his legs at the knees. That was when the fly crawled up from inside the rather dirty Roman collar to settle on the nostril of the priest nearest him, and he saw the twitch. At first he thought it was his imagination, but when it happened again he yelled for Throckton. Throckton was the squad's medic.

The young PFC burst in immediately, his rifle at the ready.

"One of them's alive. I'm sure of it!" Ron realized he was still yelling.

Quickly Throckton took a pulse behind the jaw of each priest. "This one!" he said excitedly, indicating the one whose nose the fly had found. Then more slowly he added, "But not for long. It's thready. He's lost too much blood."

"No! No!" Ron was shouting again. "I'm A-positive! You can transfuse, can't you?"

"Yes, but . . . yes." Throckton could sense Ron's excitement. "But that's not enough!" He shook his index finger in a kind of maternal admonition. "To get enough, we'd kill you to save him! By the look of it he needs four, five pints! I can't take more than one, maybe one and a half out of you, and that's dangerous, anyway!"

"Let me see!" Ron grabbed Throckton's identification tags. "No! You're A-negative!"

"So's Barrow," Throckton replied. "And Highland's AB something. Haight-Windsor's O-negative."

"O-negative!" Ron grabbed Throckton's arm. "That's universal donor, right? Can you get enough out of me and out of Haight-Windsor to keep the priest alive until we get to the airstrip at Rumuruti? That's an hour away in the Rover!"

Throckton pulled his arm away reluctantly. "But Colour Sergeant! It's not that simple! O-negative is okay, but . . . how do we know the priest's blood type matches yours? If we give him the wrong type, we'll kill him, anyway!"

"Trust me." Ron said. "Which arm? Let's get started. Then he shouted, "Barrow! Get out there and get the Rover and bring that fool wireless operator with you!"

▸ *What has made Ron Forrester confident that his A-positive blood is the same blood type as the priest who is still alive?*

35

IN SEARCH
OF ANSWERS

▼

Every window in the little studio was open as wide as possible in a vain attempt to catch whatever tired breeze might limp by from time to time. Inside, however, this arrangement produced no results. The air in the place had been hot, wet, and motionless all day. Still, at least one of Celeste Wyman's questions was answered: namely, why had Virgil Powys left every window — and the door, too — wide open when he supposedly dashed back to his house? In this heat wave, it made sense. No one was closing windows these days.

There was an answer, too, for another of Celeste's questions. Why wasn't the place air conditioned? By visiting the studio personally, by actually coming to the scene of the crime, so to speak, Celeste could see that an air conditioner would be intolerable. Too noisy. And it would box the place in. One of the studio's charms was that, despite the tight quarters, the number of windows created an impression of space. Powys claimed he had claustrophobia. Celeste certainly didn't, but she could sense what the effects would be if the sight lines were blocked.

She sat down at the table that served as a desk and looked out the large window across the room. Beyond it, over the alley and on the other side of a line of mature oak trees, traffic from Bronson Avenue superimposed its noise over the buzz and beep and chunter of the computers to her right. Side by side, on a counter that ran the length of the one wall without a window, sat a 486 tower, a Gateway 2000 4DX2, and beside it, a much more modest 386 desktop. Celeste leaned a little closer to the 486. Sixteen Meg RAM, she figured. Clockspeed of sixty-six megahertz. A lot more powerful than its immediate neighbor.

The machinery made a sharp contrast to the Chippendale reproduction table at which she was sitting, but both the table and counter shared the disarray of the studio. Stashed in every available space on the counter was a flotsam of envelopes jammed with material, the lot held in place by a Gordian knot of wires and cables and power bars that only an original installer could ever untie. On the nearest edge of the table, pens spilled out of a pewter beer stein and trailed across to a pewter envelope holder lying empty on its side. On the left edge, irregular stacks of medical reference texts were interspersed with piles of dictionaries and manuals.

Celeste lifted a heavy metal stapler from the pile of papers on the crowded working surface in front of her. The first page, and then the second, the third, and then the fourth, when she looked further, answered yet another question. Powys was obviously one of those types who worked things out on paper first and only then went to the keyboard. It was not what she would have expected. Someone with his expertise, his passion for computers, seemed more likely to work "cold," right on the keyboard with no intermediate steps.

Virgil Powys had a reputation as a computer *wunderkind*. He'd started with IBM three years ago, and after two revolutionary patents, jumped to Apple for six months and then to Wang for two before going freelance. But he wasn't doing well at freelancing. He was brilliant but erratic; he needed the discipline of an organization around him, but with his reputation for instability no one would touch him anymore. Nevertheless, when Celeste's company, Hygiolic Incorporated, retained him six weeks ago, they thought they'd made a steal. This morning, "steal" suddenly had a whole new meaning.

Celeste Wyman was Director of Research at Hygiolic. It was a company specializing in the development and production of highly advanced and complicated drugs and medicines. For months the company had been on the verge of a historic medical breakthrough. By means of computer models, they had developed — theoretically — a vaccine to protect against common cold viruses. The trouble was no one could put all the strands together; there wasn't anybody in Celeste's department who could do it. And the board of directors had so severely limited access to the models for security reasons, that, in effect, Hygiolic had been going nowhere with what could be the biggest thing since the Salk vaccine.

Yesterday, Powys had called to say he'd done it. This morning he called again, this time to say he thought the work might have been pirated, that while he'd been out for just minutes, someone had been into the studio and into the program.

Celeste leaned back in the chair and stretched, idly running both index fingers against the flyscreen behind her. There were so many questions. Should she call the police? Not yet.

Find out more first. Is it possible that Powys himself was stealing the program? That this whole break-in thing was a red herring? Not likely. It would be too hard for him to sell it. Oh, there were companies that would grab it first chance. But from Powys? No. Too easy to trace.

She leaned forward again, and put her elbows on the table. Did whoever had been into the system actually steal Hygiolic's big discovery? Yes. At the very least that had to be assumed. Espionage in medical research is as vicious as in warfare.

But then there were the truly niggling questions. Was Virgil Powys in cahoots with whoever did the pirating? Why, especially if he had put audit controls in the system that could tell him if someone had been into it, had he not encrypted the data? Used code? Powys's explanation was that Hygiolic was pushing so hard for results that using an encryption scheme good enough to protect against even a run-of-the-mill hacker would have slowed him right down. Reasonable enough, Celeste knew; she had been one of the ones pushing.

But then, at the very least, why hadn't he protected his system with a password? The answer to that was on the wall. For the third or fourth time in the past half hour, Celeste looked up at the wall above the 386. In large block letters she could see "HYGISNEEZE" written on the wallpaper with a felt-tipped pen. She shook her head. He had used a password all right! But then, hanging it out for all to see was something she did herself. So did others in her department. Not on the wallpaper though.

A noise from behind her made Celeste turn. Through the open door she could see Sean, her assistant, leaving the back door of the house and making his way across the lawn to the shed where Powys had built the studio. She counted Sean's steps: twenty-five. About twenty seconds, she calculated. Another ten to come up the stairs. Powys had said he'd gone back to the house to go to the bathroom, so that would be about thirty seconds each way. Allow, say, five minutes in the bathroom. Then he got a phone call. Long distance, he'd said, so that would be easy to verify. The call took about five minutes, supposedly, so according to Powys, he was out of the studio for ten or eleven minutes. Enough time for a pirate to dash in and copy everything? No, not at all, no matter how good. Not even if he knew where to go and how to get in.

So, was Virgil Powys out of the studio for longer than he had said he was? No doubt about it. And was he out for a longer time because he had arranged to be? Well, Celeste thought, maybe it is indeed time to involve the police. They're probably better at finding out that kind of information. At least she knew that Powys needed to be questioned.

► *Why is Celeste Wyman certain that Virgil Powys was out of the studio for longer than the time he claimed to be?*

36

VANDALISM AT THE BEL MONTE GALLERY

▼

Robbie Dexel paced back and forth on the sidewalk, forcing himself to go slowly and deliberately, at a measured pace, but his distress was obvious. Every few seconds he would stop, put his hand to his mouth, and cough hard. Then the pacing would resume. Alongside him, in the street, cars passed by in a regular rhythm. On the other side, just a few feet away, under a chestnut tree that towered over the building behind her, a uniformed police officer watched with interest. Eventually she grinned and spoke.

"Stomping back and forth like that isn't going to get them here any faster, you know. I mean, they're late. The roads are icy. Nothing we haven't encountered before."

Robbie stopped and glared hard at her. "Hey, it makes me feel better, OK? You got a problem with that? I prefer to walk and cough instead of stand and cough. Now if that bothers you then, then . . . Look, I'm sorry. It's this lousy cold. Makes me so cranky. Happens this time of year without fail. Ever since I can remember, just before before Christmas I get a cold."

Officer Dale Dunn grinned again and nodded. She moved a few steps closer.

"No problem. I'm not much good at waiting either, really. And I don't have a cold! Quite frankly, I don't see why we can't wait inside in the gallery instead of out here in the cold."

She waved at the building behind her. It was a two-story, turn-of-the-century brick structure, very tastefully renovated. The whole street was like that: restored buildings that housed boutiques, all of them upscale shops with limited hours and one-of-a-kind inventory. The facing immediately behind Dale framed a large wooden door, which in turn held a brass plaque announcing in delicate letters that the Bel Monte Gallery awaited its very special clientele on the other side.

"At least if we were inside," Dale went on, "we could look at the paintings. A lot more interesting than staring at the traffic out here."

Robbie took a deep breath, slowly, so that he wouldn't make himself cough. He spoke slowly too, trying to get a whole sentence out without having to clear his throat.

"We have to wait out here," he said, "because here is where the new witness says he was standing when he saw the job being done."

Robbie was referring to an incident at the Bel Monte Gallery that had taken place several months previously. During the night, someone had broken into the gallery through the roof, thereby defeating the security system, and had damaged a number of very valuable oil paintings by slashing them with a knife. The police had made an arrest within days, however, and at that very moment in the county jail one of the city's best known art collectors, Marc-Jean DiBeau, was being held without bail for his upcoming trial.

Dale had been the arresting officer and Robbie was the investigator from the agency that had insured the paintings. The two of them had returned to the Bel Monte site together because of a somewhat startling development. A witness had surfaced the day before, telling a story that put an entirely new twist on the case. It was their job now to question him, and they wanted to do it at the scene.

Dale pointed up the street to where a police patrol car had pulled over to the curb. "Here we are," she said. "Our witness." She lifted her eyebrows at Robbie. "Don't be shocked."

Robbie pivoted slowly and focused on the two people getting out of the car. One was a police officer, an older man, the other, well, in spite of Dale's warning, Robbie couldn't quite restrain himself.

"Him? That's the witness? He's a streetperson, a . . . a bum!"

Dale shrugged her shoulders. "Think about it. Who else is going to be out here at two o'clock in the morning? This is a commercial district. There's nobody living here. By the way, his name is Patchy Lomax."

"Patchy?"

"Look at the clothes. What would you call him?"

As Patchy and his escort came closer, Robbie swore he was looking at a circus clown. There was barely a spot on Patchy's clothes that was not covered by squares and rectangles of every imaginable texture and hue. Perched on top of this kaleidoscope was a mass of crinkly gray hair that grew up and down and out, covering every facial feature except for a very red, round nose that moved like some kind of battery-powered toy.

Patchy wasted no time. "Up there. Up there at the window, 'at's where I seen 'er." A skinny, nicotine-stained finger appeared out of a rainbow sleeve and pointed at a window on the second floor of the Bel Monte Gallery. "'At's where I seen her do it. Slash them pictures. Big woman. Tall. Lotsa hair. Long. An' I seen 'er. No question."

Robbie frowned. One of the partners who owned the gallery was a tall woman with long hair. He started to talk but the coughing took over, so Dale asked the obvious questions.

"OK, so you saw a woman at the window, but you're going to have to do a lot better than that. What were you doing here at two o'clock in the morning? And it's dark then. You can see in the dark maybe?"

Patchy raised his red nose in the air. Another skinny, yellow-brown finger appeared, this time pointed accusingly at Dale. Before Patchy could speak, Robbie interjected.

"What we want to know more than anything is why you didn't tell us all this four months ago when it happened. Why now?"

The finger was joined by its colleagues, the grimy hand now held out like a traffic cop, first at Robbie, then at Dale. Patchy lifted his red nose even further. With great dignity, he turned to the bus shelter a few feet from where they were standing. "In here, lady cop." He took a step and turned to Robbie. "You too. It's answers you want? Then one at a time. We start in here."

Both Robbie and Dale followed obediently; neither of them caught the smile on the face of the older officer.

"I was in here," Patchy announced once he was fully satisfied he had everyone in place and fully attentive. "'Cause you could tell it was gonna rain hard."

Robbie stole a quick glance at Dale. Patchy was right about that. It had rained the night of the break-in, a harsh downpour that, according to the weather office, had begun at 2:15 AM and lasted about ten minutes.

"Now yuz look up there." The finger came out again, leading them back to the second floor. "That winda'. Right b'tween them branches there. Ya see? 'At's where I seen 'er, 'cause the lights is on all the time in that buildin'. Leastways all night they are. Ya knew that too, didn't ya, lady cop? Tryin' t' fool old Patchy, weren't ya?"

Through the labyrinth of hair, Robbie could see a pair of dark eyes gleaming triumphantly. He took a long breath very slowly and said, "But this doesn't explain why you waited all this time to tell anybody what you saw."

The gleaming eyes bored into the young investigator's. "Well, young fella, it just happens that I don't read the art news every day. How'm I supposed to know that somebody has ruined a painting? So far's I know, she mighta been doin' that 'cause she was supposed to. Ya know, cuttin' it up and then callin' it art.

"Anyways, I didn't know nothin' about this until I met yer Mark John Dee Bo fella down at th'county. Some right interestin' people in that jail from time t' time. Anyways, ya got the wrong guy. It was a woman done it. I seen her."

Without waiting for a response, Patchy Lomax turned and left the shelter, heading back to the police car that had brought him. Dale Dunn, meanwhile, continued to stare at the window, as did Robbie Dexel, each waiting for the other to speak.

It was Robbie who finally broke the silence. "Pretty solid, you agree?"

Dale nodded.

"I almost bought it," Robbie continued. "You too?"

Dale nodded again.

► *Apparently, neither Robbie Dexel nor Dale Dunn have been convinced by Patchy Lomax's story. Why not? What's wrong with Patchy's version?*

37

TWO SHOTS
WERE FIRED

▼

The young policeman at the gate stiffened when he recognized the senior officer getting out of the car that had just pulled up. Instinctively, a hand went to his throat where his tie hung loosely around an open top button. Inspector Vince Pogor was a stickler for proper dress no matter what the weather, and the young constable knew it was too late now to rebutton his collar.

"You look like that when the media was here?" Vince was also known for getting right to the point.

"No. No, sir!" The young man's face, already soaking from the heat of the sun, began sweating even harder.

Vince lifted his hands to his hips. The gesture reminded him that he himself wasn't in uniform at all, that in fact he was in a T-shirt and shorts — kind of ratty ones to boot.

"Okay. Okay." he said. "Just . . . Look, you know the

regulation. Tie on or tie off. Not that halfway stuff. Now. Where's the shooting site? That it up there?"

"Yes sir!" The officer was so relieved he absently brought out a none-too-clean handkerchief to wipe his face. "Just around the corner of the building there. You'll see the yellow tape."

For a second or two, Vince toyed with the idea of going back to division headquarters to change clothes. The incident with the constable's tie had made him self-conscious about his own dress. In the end he decided not to. The media had been and gone, especially the TV cameras. Besides — he looked at his watch — the incident was already six hours old.

Vince was calling it an incident, not a *crime*, for the time being anyway. The evidence so far pointed in that direction. It was an accidental shooting, but a dicey one because of the victim. The dead man, Big Dino, was well-known to Vince, in fact to just about everyone on the police force, especially the anti-racket squad which Vince headed up. Big Dino had roots deep in organized crime. Until this morning. This morning Big Dino had gone down with two bullets in the middle of his chest just outside the rear entrance to Galahad Storage. He'd been shot from inside the building by a security guard.

"Ah . . . sir?" It was the constable. He'd taken his tie off. "Up there? Around the corner? Sergeant King . . . ah . . . he's waiting for you."

Vince grunted, just a wee bit embarrassed, then began to walk toward the rear of the building. He was glad to stretch his legs for he'd had a long drive. Officially, Vince was on vacation. The first two weeks of August were always his. That morning before anyone else in the family was awake, he'd taken a giant plate of bacon and perogies out to the deck of his cottage, despite the threat of rain, and had just snapped on the portable to listen to *The World at Eight* when the telephone rang, summoning him away from his beloved Lake Muskoka.

He'd headed down to the city right away, but changing out of the shorts and T-shirt did not even cross his mind. The heat wave that stretched from the American Midwest right up to the Arctic was so fierce that even the thought of full-length trousers made him sweat. And the heat was getting worse, too. On his way south, the dull sky that had covered most of Eastern North America that morning reneged on its promise of rain and cooler weather, completely contradicting the weather forecasters. By the time Vince could see Toronto in the distance, the sky had turned blue and cloudless and the day was flatiron hot.

Not a day to spend walking on confounded asphalt, he thought, turning the corner where yellow boundary tape squared off a section of empty lot. He hardly noticed the tape at first, or even how much hotter it was on this side of the building. What caught his attention instead was the overwhelming, relentless noise from the traffic on the Queen Elizabeth Way. Ten lanes of speeding, bumper-to-bumper racket so loud he didn't hear Jack King until the third yell.

"Vinny! Vince! In here! Outa the sun!"

Vince ducked under the tape, stepped carefully over the chalk outline of a body, and walked through the only open door. It had a small sign that said "EMPLOYEES ONLY." Jack King was standing inside. His tie was pulled down and he had two buttons undone. Jack began to speak immediately.

"It was like this," he said. Vince realized that Jack had been waiting in the heat for some time and had no intention of dawdling through his report. He wanted to get back to headquarters and air conditioning.

"The guard sat here, his back to the door you just came through." He pointed to a battered metal chair and an old wooden table with a deck of greasy playing cards on top. "Says he was watching the front. That makes sense 'cause that's where all the break-ins have been coming through. Especially the one two days ago where one a' the other guards got beat up so bad."

Vince raised his eyebrows but said nothing. Jack went on. "Then all of a sudden, he says there's this dark shadow over him. From behind. From the doorway. He whips around. The sun's in his face. There's an awful big guy there so . . . *Boom! Boom!* Two in the chest."

"Sounds a bit trigger happy, don't you think?" Vince spoke for the first time.

"Yeah. But don't forget the guy was scared," Jack answered. "I mean, there's been so much trouble here. All the break-ins. They had that fire where the guy was trapped in a room. Then there's that guard who was beat up. Word is he'll never walk again. Can't say I really blame the guard for shooting. And Dino. He's a big guy. 'Sides, he had no business back here. We think he's a renter here. Least he had a key in his pocket. We're checkin' that right now. Anyway, how's the guard supposed to know? As it is, the place doesn't open to customers till nine o'clock. And not through this door." Jack was pointing out the door to the east. Through the opening Vince could see the skyline of the city in the distance and the surface of Lake Ontario shimmering in the brightness of midday.

I don't know, Jack," he said. "It's still too neat. This door was open then?"

"Propped open," Jack answered. "Just like it is now. Haven't you noticed how hot it is in here? I can believe the guard when he says the door had to be open. And that means he couldn't hear anything either. With the highway traffic at that time of the morning."

Vince nodded. "Yeah, I guess so. Sounds like accidental shooting all right. There's only one thing that's not right."
"Yeah? What's that?" Jack King wanted to know.

► *What is the flaw in the security guard's story that Vince Pogor is referring to?*

38

INVESTIGATING THE FAILED DRUG BUST

▼

There was still a bit of snow on the ground, small piles of it wrapped around the base of the trees that lined both sides of the path. There was even more of it just a few feet off the path where, years before, the Department of Parks and Recreation had made yet another attempt to create the illusion of a natural environment in the middle of the city. Betty Stadler rather enjoyed the irony of it all. The trees grew and the snow fell, and every winter weekend enthusiastic urbanites, dressed better than Scott's polar expedition, pretended they were confronting the forces of nature — without ever straying off the path.

Still, phony as it was, Gallenkirk Park was better than no park at all. A lot better. And Betty Stadler, Lieutenant Elizabeth Stadler, recently appointed to Internal Affairs, had to admit she preferred to be out here, especially if the alternative was another smoke-filled committee room back at headquarters. Years before, more years than she cared to acknowledge, when she was the force's first female officer, Gallenkirk Park had been in her precinct. She had been part of an experimental bicycle patrol group that covered the park, along with an adjacent public housing project that had been put together during the Eisenhower administration with a lot less planning than Parks and Rec had put into the trees.

She'd loved the park then, and did even more so now. The trees were mature now, and had attracted some wildlife. There was irony in that too. Nature, "red in tooth and claw," as Tennyson had put it, had returned to the middle of the city. But the fauna was far less dangerous than the wildlife that dominated the drug trade in the high-rise projects next door, a trade that contaminated everyone and everything that came into even the remotest contact with it.

Betty was acutely aware of the ultimate irony in her situation this morning. She was here in one of her favorite places in the whole city, but only because it might provide a setting for one of her least favorite responsibilities: investigating whether a cop might be dirty.

Not a rookie this time, not like the last time when her investigation turned up a scandalous mess that traced back to the police academy. The one this time was an officer with some fifteen years' tenure. He had spent the last three years undercover on the "old clothes" detail, living in shelters and on the street, soaking up information and cheap wine. In a way she felt sorry for the cops on "old clothes." They volunteered for it all right; no one forced them, even though it could be a real career boost because it was one of those ugly but very important police jobs that few wanted. But so many of the personnel on this detail eventually developed a real problem staying level. Either they became fanatics, crusaders, so that Betty and her team ended up investigating them for unnecessary force or illegal entrapment, or else they became so soiled by the world they dealt with that they became part of it.

Betty had met Officer Dana only once before. He'd been a member of the mounted patrol then, a coveted assignment, and she couldn't understand why he'd volunteered to transfer out. It could have been the divorce, she thought when reading his file. The break-up had been messy, and for Dana, excruciating. His two kids now lived with their mother over a thousand miles away. Yet the shift to "old clothes" seemed to be the right thing to do, at least in the beginning. In his first year he'd turned over enough good stuff to earn three citations. But his markers slowed after that, and in the third year his file showed such a sharp decline that Internal Affairs had flagged it. A few hours ago that attention had made Betty notice something in the morning reports that, most times, would have slid through without even a raised eyebrow.

The night before, the narcotics squad had pulled off a major bust that was coordinated across several points in the city. It had taken months of preparation, and although the squad had proceeded with its customary secrecy and, in Betty's opinion, utter lack of cooperation from the rest of the force, it was impossible to hide the fact that something big was going down. By the time of the bust, the where and when, and even the who, were common knowledge. Even so, the squad went ahead with every expectation of success and everything went as planned, except for one small and, on the surface, entirely peripheral part: a failed arrest in Gallenkirk Park. The only collar the squad made there was a wino who so far had refused to talk.

According to the detective from narcotics — he was the only one who saw it firsthand, other than Dana and the drug dealers who had gotten away — the potential collars had been approaching from three different directions for their meet. When they were almost within speaking distance of one another, the sound of someone walking through the leaves just off the path tipped them off. Although it was too dark to see much, the dealers were taking no chances and scattered. The approaching person, the one who scared them off, turned out to be just a wino, but by then the operation was dead. The wino, who Betty knew to be Officer Dana, had been charged with obstructing police business. It was a sour-grapes charge at best and, if the stories all checked out, one that would be dropped quickly to save everyone embarrassment.

Had Betty not come out here this morning to confirm her suspicions, it all might have ended there, but now she knew there was dirt. More than she'd originally suspected, because now there were two cops to investigate.

She took a deep breath, and turned completely around for a last long look. She was sure she'd seen a robin at the top of an oak tree just ahead. An early returner, but a good sign. Further ahead she saw the sun trying to push its way through the clouds. Another good sign. After a week of almost steady drizzle and gloom, some sunshine would be welcome.

► *Why has Lieutenant Betty Stadler determined that there are now two cops to investigate?*

39

A Double Assassination
at "The Falls"

▼

O ut of habit, Vince Moro reached up to clean a fingerprint
off the rear-view mirror, before adjusting it down a bit so
he could see out the back. Then he picked up the envelope
that was balled up and stuffed behind the gearshift in the
center console, and put it in the glove compartment.

Don't know why I'm doing this, Vince thought as he
reached over to pick up a pair of cigarette butts from the
floor on the passenger side. "I really don't know why." This
time he said it out loud, while throwing the two butts out the
passenger side window — or what was left of it.

The fact was, Vince was compulsively neat, and nothing
bothered him more than a messy car. It was a point of
personal pride that no vehicle left Vince's Auto Body dirty.
Not ever, no matter how tiny or insignificant the repair.

But this car? There was surely no point in cleaning it.

Certainly no point in trying to repair it. The thing was a write-off, and Vince was simply here to tow it away to the wrecking yard. The front and back of the car were okay. In fact, the dash had that spotless, uncluttered look Vince always liked in cars that had just left a rental agency. And the shelf beneath the back window was pleasantly free of the invariable accumulation of clutter and junk.

The front seats, however, and the front windows, the center post, even the roof above the front seat: they were a different matter. The killers had sprayed so many bullets over these areas that the headrest on the passenger seat had been chewed right off, leaving a frothy stump of stuffing, its original whiteness now covered in drying blood. A few minutes ago Vince had overheard one of the investigators — he was sure it was one of the CIA guys — say that both victims had taken over twenty rounds in the upper torso.

"You the guy from Hertz?"

The voice in Vince's ear startled him, but he strove not to show it. His hearing more than his sight told him it was the sergeant from the highway patrol. Although the two men had met before, more than once, the sergeant never, ever recognized Vince. Or pretended not to. Vince didn't like him.

"I have been *retained* by Hertz," Vince said, getting out of the car with deliberate slowness. "I'm here to take the car. It's cleared to go?"

He folded his arms and leaned against the car. It was the same sergeant all right. A tall fellow, at least a head taller than Vince. And he had the annoying habit of standing so close when he talked that the other person had to lean back to look up, or else step backward. That's why Vince leaned against the car.

"Not yet," the sergeant replied as he took off his hat and wiped his forehead with his sleeve. Vince was sure he was actually moving closer.

"Not yet," the policeman said again. "There has to be some —"

"Okay, Sergeant, if you will, please! The photographer can use you now."

Vince whipped around quickly. It was not a voice he'd heard before, today or at any time. The accent was British, and as the speaker approached, Vince knew he was a complete stranger. That was not surprising; the place was crawling with investigators. The CIA was here; Vince knew that for sure. And the RCMP. Two of them had come from Ottawa in a Lear jet. And the whole scene had been shut down while they waited for two more people to come up from Buffalo. No one had told Vince directly, but he could tell they were in charge. Now who the British guy was, Vince had no idea at all, but certainly he was connected with the affair.

Just before dawn, two diplomats from the French consulate in Buffalo, New York, had crossed into Canada over the Rainbow Bridge at Niagara Falls. Not more than a few minutes later, while stopped at a traffic light, they were shot down in an absolute storm of machine-gun bullets. Then their bodies had been dragged out of the car and, as though to send a message, laid side by side in front of the car and sprayed with bullets again. The assassins had escaped.

"Excuse me, sir." The British accent was very polite. A great deal more polite than the sergeant. "Who are . . . oh, yes. Forgive me!"

The man peered closer at the badge that dangled from Vince's shirt pocket and proclaimed CLEARANCE — SITE ONLY.

"You're the gentleman here to tow away the vehicle, aren't you? If you don't mind waiting just a few minutes more. Some photos we need. It would be convenient if you didn't drive over the outlines there."

He pointed to the chalk outlines on the pavement in front of the car, which marked where the bodies of the diplomats had lain. The sergeant was now lying down beside the longer one. It was clear his dignity was wounded and Vince was just beginning to enjoy that when the accent said, "There's one more thing, actually. It's frightfully awkward, I know, but you . . . uh . . . you are just about the size of one of the victims. Do you . . . uh . . . would you mind awfully lying down there like the sergeant? I'm sorry, I can't really explain why, but it will help us. A reconstruct-the-scene sort of thing, you see."

For an instant, but only an instant, Vince wondered if maybe he wasn't being had. But the sergeant was already lying on the pavement, and the situation was hardly one for humor, macabre or otherwise. He nodded and went to the front of the car, glad now that he'd left on his coveralls to drive out here, and lay down beside the other outline.

"A bit embarrassing, this," Vince muttered to the sergeant. There was no response. The sergeant was definitely embarrassed and had no wish to discuss the fact. "All in the interests of justice," Vince continued, determined to make it known that he could make light of the indignity. "By the way," he said, "would it help if you knew which one of them was driving when they were shot?"

The sergeant sat bolt upright so suddenly that the photographer yelled. "How do you know?" the policeman asked.

▶ *How does Vince Moro know who was driving?*

40

A DECISION AT RATTLESNAKE POINT

▼

The cable screamed over the large pulley at the end of the mobile crane, launching a massive assault on the morning quiet. The arm of the crane was fully extended to reach over the brow of Rattlesnake Point, for the body had to come up from two hundred feet below. It was the distance more than the weight that made the equipment work so hard.

As he talked to Trevor Hawkes, the young doctor from the medical examiner's office watched the big machine with a wary eye. Perry Provato had ridden down and then back up via the crane within the past hour, and he was not at all impressed by what he saw, now that he was watching from the top.

"It's like I said, Trevor," he pointed sideways with his thumb at the body that was now coming over the edge of the cliff. Trussed up in a rescue basket, it bounced and swayed at the end of the cable like some macabre yo-yo that had got stuck on the way to the spool. "Like I said, I might do a bit better at the morgue this afternoon, but I'll take bets that the death took place six to eight hours ago."

Trevor nodded and looked at his watch. "So . . . 'tween 1:00 and 3:00 AM. Makes sense." He motioned to the crane operator and then pointed to a clear spot beside the guard rail. "Highway patrol reported the car at, let's see, 4:46. Then . . ."

He waved frantically at the crane operator. "No! No! This side! Over here!" he yelled, pointing with both arms to the spot beside the rail.

"So," he said, his voice returning immediately to normal, "first light was 5:20. Patrol confirmed a body down in the scrub about ten minutes after that. And you went down, what? About 8:00. An hour ago, right?"

"Yeah, eight," Perry replied. "Never done that before. Go down on a cable, I mean. Can't say I want to again either! You just stand on the big grab hook and hang on! I mean, even the dead guy gets strapped into a basket.

"And what a mess when I got down there! He's a big guy. Not lanky like you, but a big one. Just think of the acceleration by the time he hit!"

Perry shook his head; his adrenalin was still pumping. "I remember this sicko physics teacher we had in high school. Liked to give us problems with falling bodies. She should try this one!"

Trevor looked at the body, lying finally where he had directed. Despite Perry's comment, it appeared remarkably intact. After a two-hundred-foot fall, all the parts were still there. In fact the face was almost unscathed. Only the big belly seemed pushed oddly to one side, and the suspenders on that side had come off. Trevor could see that the neck was broken, likely the spine, too, in several places.

"One thing, Perry, before you go. In your, uh, your uh, uh . . ." Trevor was trying to find the right word. Perry was so young. He settled on "experience" anyway. "In your experience, uh . . . well, there's a note on the driver's seat in the car there." He knew that Perry was looking at the silver-gray Lincoln Town Car behind them. It was parked in perfect parallel on the verge between the road and the guard rail. "Can't be sure, of course, till we go inside, but my guess is it's a suicide note. Now, what makes a guy do himself in like that when there's . . . ?"

"You mean," Perry took the lead, "why didn't he just let the car run and go to sleep? Or overdose? Or something softer like that? I dunno. I guess some of them just want to be more dramatic. I know that some jumpers do it because they really want to punish themselves. But it's a lot quicker the way he did it! Then there's always the —"

The rest of what Perry had to say was erased by the scream of the cable. Both men looked to see Trevor's rookie partner, Ashlynne Walmsley, on her way over the brow of Rattlesnake Point. Unlike the other passengers so far, it was clear she was enjoying herself completely. Ashlynne waved a camera at Trevor as soon as the operator set her down.

"Lots of shots," she said. "Covered everything."

Trevor pointed to the body. "Get a couple there," he said, "then the car from several angles. And . . . just a minute!" He knelt beside the body. "Make sure you witness this." He patted the dead man's pockets and then reached into one of them and extracted a small ring of keys. "Just in case some jackass lawyer ever wants to know in court where we got these."

"Trust me," Ashlynne said and began snapping shots of the car.

Trevor, meanwhile, waved goodbye to the retreating Perry and went to the driver's door of the Lincoln. He inserted a key and turned it sharply. All four door locks popped open simultaneously, along with — to his complete surprise — the trunk lid. He reached for the door handle, then shrugged and went to the back of the car instead. Except for a CD player and a small rack of discs, the cavernous trunk was empty and very clean. With his pen, Trevor spread the discs apart and craned his neck to read the titles only to bump into Ashlynne who was peering over his shoulder.

"George Strait, Randy Travis, Dolly Parton," she read aloud. "Reba McIntyre. All country. Well, he's consistent anyway. Kitty Wells! Who's Kitty Wells?"

The question made Trevor feel his age so he ignored it. "Time to go inside," he said. "There's nothing here. You go to the passenger side and open up. Just witness what I do. I got a funny feeling we're going to have to explain a lot about this one."

"You mean," Ashlynne asked, "You think it's fishy that a guy would park his car so neat if he's going to jump? And lock it, too? And take the keys?"

Trevor didn't answer. He simply walked around to the driver's door and opened it after Ashlynne had done as she was instructed. The paper on the seat was of a standard memo-pad size. Again using his pen, Trevor turned it over. It was a note. It said simply:

Try to get me *now*.

A.

"Want my flashlight?" Ashlynne asked when she saw Trevor tilt up the steering column and bend himself in to look under the seat.

He just shook his head.

"Then is it okay if I see where the radio stations are pre-set? And, uh, like, Trevor . . . shouldn't the fingerprint people be here?"

Trevor Hawkes maneuvered himself back out of the car and stretched his long frame. He looked over at the crane operator who had sidled as close as he dared to the body.

"Good thinking on the radio stations," he said finally. "And yeah, you're right. Let's give the forensic bunch their shot. There won't be any prints though. Whoever murdered this guy isn't that dumb."

► *What has finally convinced Trevor Hawkes that this is a murder case?*

41

WHEN THE OXYGEN RAN OUT

▼

The room was sparsely furnished and, as a result, uninviting. There was only one place to sit: a single, straight-backed chair, a refugee from an uncomfortable dining room suite, that sat disapprovingly in one corner, just to the left of the window. Under the window itself, an old-fashioned hot-water radiator hissed softly. More or less in the center stood a burnished walnut end table. It was highly polished but had no gleam, and it didn't match the chair. Behind the little table, there was a floor lamp with a shade that may once have been ivory-colored but had aged now to a russet orange. Altogether, though, there was enough furniture for the room. More would have made the place seem crowded. With or without the dead man in the wheelchair.

As it was, the dark wooden bookshelves, the deep brownish-red rug, and the heavy, flocked wallpaper made the room appear even smaller than it was. The first thing she would do if it were her place, Fran Singleton decided, would be to lighten it up. Get rid of the wallpaper first. Maybe even paint the shelves, although that would take some courage, for they were genuine oak. Solid too, no veneer. And the rug. To her, the color choice, especially in a room like this, was almost a criminal act.

Fran always redecorated her surroundings when she found herself in an unpleasant situation. It took her mind off grim details that she didn't want to deal with. In this case, it was the not-unexpected demise of the late Humbert Latham.

She was not here by choice.

"All you've got to do is sign the death certificate," Lenny Stracwyz had pleaded over the telephone. Lenny was the county coroner and a classmate of Fran's from med school. He was in the Bahamas on vacation and had asked Fran to do him this favor, for he had no intention of leaving the beach to return to the cold of Toronto in January.

"Just sign the death certificate for me," he had repeated when Fran hesitated. "There's no question he's dead, from what I gather. Natural causes. Simple as can be. It just needs a signature. You don't have to do anything else — except, uh, uh, well, maybe you'd better make a few notes just in case I have to call an inquest."

Fran had tried to say something at that point but Lenny Stracwyz cut her off.

"Just sign," he said. "Please? Make it official? So I don't have to come home? You don't even have to do time of death; that's done already. OK?"

The mention of a possible inquest had made Fran more hesitant than ever, but the plaintiveness of Lenny's voice had pushed away her natural reluctance. She had wanted to remind him that she was a pediatrician and didn't "do death," but in spite of that she found herself, less than an hour later, holding the cold wrist of Humbert Latham, confirming the nonexistent pulse.

The body of the old man still sat, bent slightly forward, in the wheelchair where he had died. His silver hair, always so perfectly groomed, reflected the lamp's wan glow, lending an impressive dignity to his death pose. Except for the slightly odd position, and the bit of drool that had dried along his chin and on the lapel of his blazer, Humbert Latham looked much as he must have when he'd been wheeled into the room yesterday afternoon, but somehow, more peaceful. There was less pain in his face than Fran remembered from the last time she had seen him. That was after the stroke. And the hands with their clawlike gnarl — she particularly remembered the hands because her own patient, Latham's great-grandson, was terrified of them — their once frightening, crippled grip seemed to be quite relaxed now. In a sense, Humbert Latham almost looked relieved that the oxygen had run out and he could finally let go.

Fran checked the oxygen bottle under the seat of the wheelchair and then followed all the tubes and checked each connection. They were all properly in place and intact.

"Sergeant Hong from homicide says it ran out between three and four this morning and the forensic specialist says he stopped breathing about fifteen minutes after that." It was the voluble rookie cop assigned to guard the scene. Sergeant Hong had not spent much time in the room. He'd simply ordered that everything remain untouched and had headed off to headquarters to coordinate the search for Latham's night nurse.

"Too bad, really. The poor old guy." The young policeman was still talking. "Lousy way to go even if it looks like he wasn't going to be around much longer anyway. I mean, you're totally helpless and you depend on someone to change your oxygen, and she doesn't show up. I mean, Jeez. Then the day nurse — I mean, like, she's the one who started all this — she's the one that finds him dead this morning!"

Fran knew the details and tried to ignore the prattle.

The day nurse regularly wheeled Humbert Latham into this room in the late afternoon so that he could enjoy the winter sunset through the west-facing window. At least everyone speculated that he enjoyed the sunset. The stroke had taken away Latham's ability to communicate. The nurse had left him alone there as she did every day at this time, and then had left the house five minutes early. Latham's valet, a man with a reputation for ironfisted control, had given her permission to do so, and had also arranged for the night nurse to come in early. It was the night nurse's job to take the old man down the hall to his bedroom, connect a fresh bottle of oxygen, and prepare him for sleep. But the night nurse had never shown up, and as yet had not been located.

"And that valet, Mr. Latham's 'gentleman'?" The policeman was leaning closer to Fran now, trying without realizing it to capture her full attention by hovering over her. "I mean, he's always here, right? Anyway he's supposed to be. But what does he do? He has a car accident! With that big Rolls. Just goes to show you, a patch of ice don't respect the make of your car. Anyway, so he gets taken to the hospital, all woozy and can't talk. So poor old Mr. Latham's got nobody. No nurse, no valet . . ."

Fran turned and leaned into the young policeman's face. He had been saying "val-ette," and that bothered her almost as much as his interference.

"It's 'val-AY.' Like the letter 'A.' French. And I know all this."

She turned to the window and took a breath, surprised by her vehemence. The morning sun was now reflecting off the windows on the building across the street, and the beauty and promise of it calmed her. Slowly, and just slightly self-conscious, she turned back to the officer.

"There's a security guard on the grounds at night, isn't there?" The more the thought took hold of her the more she forgot her annoyance. "There is, if I remember correctly. Seems to me he gave me a hard time once when I came on a house call."

The policeman looked at her uncomprehendingly.

"Because," she went on, excited now, "unless he too was missing last night — seems like everybody else was — I'd bet Sergeant Hong will want to know if he's the same one that's on every night."

► *Why is Fran Singleton interested in this information about the security guard?*

42

THE CASE OF THE SCALPEL MURDER

▼

A ny other town but Shorthorn would have written off old
Doc Virgil long ago as an out-and-out certifiable nut
case. Even by the most relaxed standards he was more than
just eccentric. For one thing he made house calls, which to
some of his colleagues was eccentric in itself. He made them,
however, in the company of a pet skunk! The little beast
didn't stay out in Doc's big Chrysler either; it accompanied
him like a consultant, right into the patient's bedroom.

Another issue was Doc's waiting room. It was a greenhouse. During office hours, patients fought their way
through a labyrinth of palm leaves, schefflera and saxifraga
sarmentosa to respond to Doc Virgil's shout of "Next!" He
did not have a receptionist, officially. Nor a nurse.

Just being able to hear "Next!" was a problem in itself
in the greenhouse. Doc loved country music — very loud

country music. He had a theory that his plants did too, and that they grew especially well to the sound of fiddles and steel guitars. No one trying to answer the call of "Next!" ever disputed this.

Yet some of Doc's notions had had other effects. He was a fanatic about dietary control of diabetes. Because of his relentless experimentation he had made some breakthroughs, which had been published and reprinted several times in the medical journals.

Perhaps the most serious matter, however, was Doc's drinking. To people outside Shorthorn, and to the few locals who eschewed his ministrations, Doc Virgil was a drunk. To everyone else he simply had a problem, and the villagers adjusted to it in the same way they had adjusted to the greenhouse, to the Ranch Boys at too many decibels and to the skunk.

It was simple. No one in Shorthorn got sick on Thursdays. Thursday was Doc's day off. He faithfully celebrated that weekly recurrence by tying one on, which always culminated in Police Chief Gary Westlake carrying the little man from the back seat of the huge, old Chrysler at about 2:00 AM, and laying him out in gentle repose in the greenhouse.

Of late, Chief Westlake had been especially careful while tiptoeing in with Doc, for fear of waking Petty. Petty — her real name was Petunia — was Doc's housekeeper or nurse or former mistress or even wife; no one knew for sure. Petty was no shrinking violet and, despite her diabetes, had a bottomless well of energy when it came to expressions of temper. Her battles with Doc were legendary, and she was to be avoided at moments like these. In fact, most of the people in Shorthorn avoided her, period. But without saying so. She was just one more element they were willing to adjust to because of old Doc. No one complained about her — or, indeed about anything regarding Doc Virgil — because every family in the village at one time or another had had reason to be grateful to him. With his unorthodox methods — perhaps because of them — he had touched everyone in Shorthorn.

Not least of all Gary Westlake. That's why he sat so forlornly right now behind the wheel of Doc's car. It was dark out on the Fourth Concession, but the combined red-and-white flashes from his patrol car — Shorthorn's only one — and from the regional ambulance were continuous enough for him to see the bloodstains on the passenger seat. There were even more where Petunia's head had lain on the floor. They were clearly visible amid the unbelievable pile of paper towels, envelopes, and empty cat-food packages. With his pen, Gary moved aside a chocolate-bar wrapper and some crumpled tissues to look at the ooze. She had bled a long time.

He was interrupted by Mel Hehn, his partner on Shorthorn's two-man force.

"That forensic fella' from th' region says it's okay t' move the car now." Mel stuck his head almost inside the driver's window. "Says they got everything they need."

Gary had been waiting for that. He reached to find the adjuster under the seat so that he could move it ahead to reach the pedals.

"Where are they taking Petty's body?" he asked Mel. "I want to see it again myself before Doc wakes up."

Doc Virgil was stretched out on the back seat in a Thursday stupor. He was covered with blood too, and in his hand was the scalpel that had finished Petty.

"Hospital, I guess," Mel replied. "I'll ask 'em. Uh . . . where you gonna put Doc?"

"The cell," Gary said. "At least till he wakes up."

Shorthorn had a single cell in the basement of the town hall cum police station and library.

"Tell that fellow from forensic I'll wait in my office. If I don't get this car out of here right now the whole town will be snooping through it."

He turned the ignition key and, along with the motor, everything in the car roared to life: wipers, air conditioner, lights. From the specially mounted rear speakers, the Rolling Stones nearly lifted Gary's hat. It took him a minute to adjust everything.

"Mel!" he called to his partner, who had turned to walk away. "Mel, I've got to arrest old Doc all right. I don't want to, but I have to. Still I don't think he did it. I've got at least three reasons to doubt it. You and I are going to have to dig deeper on this one."

► *What are the three items that have made Gary Westlake doubtful of Doc Virgil's guilt?*

43

SPY VERSUS SPY

▼

"In counterespionage, Hauptmann August, we are not interested in spies as much as we are in spy *networks*."

"I understand, Herr Oberst, but . . ." Ernst August tried to break in, but it was Oberst Dietrich Staat's favorite lecture, and he was not about to have its delivery interrupted by an officer of inferior rank.

"So if we act upon your suggestion, Hauptmann," he continued, "we will succeed in doing what? We will arrest this . . . this Kopenick of yours, and what will we have? Nothing but another foot soldier, another pair of eyes and ears that can be replaced just like that!" Oberst Staat snapped his fingers. It was a constant habit of his, one he indulged in almost as frequently as asking himself rhetorical questions.

Hauptmann Ernst August yielded to the defeat that crept from the back of his brain, ran over his skull, and fixed his face in an immobile, neutral expression. There was no other way but to endure it. He had been through this lecture before: the same words, the same intonations, the same gestures. The same stinking cloud of cigarette smoke. It made him wonder yet again what devious gremlin of fate had conspired to have him transferred from the Abwehr, the military intelligence service led by his hero, Admiral Canaris, to the Sicherheitdienst, the infamous SD. It was bad enough that he had to admit to his fellow career officers in the Wermacht that he was now working for that madman, Heydrich. Worse was that his superior officer was Dietrich Staat, the most short-sighted drone in the service.

Staat's lecture went on. "Stuttgart is full of little traitors like your Kopenick, full of closet communists. I understand your enthusiasm and I commend it. Your skill, too, in identifying Kopenick. But what does he mean to us?" The colonel paused to squash out his Gauloise and insert another into the end of his ivory cigarette holder. He did not offer one to August. "It may mean one less instrument in the network for a very short while. But before long, he will be replaced. No, in counterespionage we must ask ourselves . . ."

Staat made an elaborate show of lighting the fresh cigarette with a table lighter on his desk. "You realize of course, Hauptmann, what would be of interest, what would be most useful . . ." Staat had forgotten the question he was going to ask and inadvertently, almost got right to the point, ". . . what would be most useful would be to find out who Kopenick's *cutout* is. Now. What would that do for us?"

Ernst August swallowed noisily. He was struggling to keep his mouth shut. The last time he'd endured this lecture, which was during the second time he had reported Kopenick's activities, Staat had laboriously explained "cutout" to him, as though both did not already know well that a cutout's role was to act as a protective connection between an agent and various subagents. The practice preserved security for the agent since, most of the time, a subagent never even learned the identity of his or her agent.

"If we knew who the cutout is, we could follow him. And then! And *then*!" Staat was reaching a plateau in his monologue. Ernst knew that either he would end it here, or God forbid, branch out in another direction. Before either could happen, Hauptmann Ernst August jumped in.

"Most astute as usual, Herr Oberst. You see, I know who the cutout is. Also, I know how they communicate. If you want to see them together and see how Kopenick passes the messages, we will have to go now while it is raining. If their pattern remains as consistent as it has been, they will rendezvous shortly near the Stiftskirche. At 1730 hours."

Luckily for Ernst August, his outburst coincided with one of Staat's elaborate inhalings. The officer core had been very much influenced in its smoking habits of late by French movies. But what Staat had just heard stopped all the mannerisms. And the lecture.

"You have his cutout?" The Oberst did not realize his mouth was agape.

"Yes, Oberst Staat. His name is Traugott Waechter. Swiss. At least he has a Swiss passport."

"Aha, a Swiss passport! Now what does that mean? It means . . ."

"Yes, Herr Oberst. He travels back and forth once a week. Stuttgart to Bern. I suspect that it is because of this Waechter that you — that *we* have not been successful with the radio location equipment. I believe that in Stuttgart, at least, *Rote Kapelle* makes very little use of radios. With Waechter available as a courier, there is no need."

For the very first time, Oberst Dietrich Staat was silent.

His mouth stayed open, but there were no words. His cigarette burned away unnoticed at the end of the holder. The mention of *Rote Kapelle* often had that effect on German intelligence.

To the SD and the Abwehr, and the Gestapo, too, the *Rote Kapelle* or "Red Orchestra" was a cause of profound embarrassment. It was a highly successful Soviet operation, a network that, especially in the first years of the war, sent amazingly accurate, thorough, and extensive reports to Moscow on German war production, military maneuvers, and even some of the long-range planning of the general staff. Many of the agents at the bottom of the chain — subagents — were ideological communists, a great number of them German, some Swiss, and some, like Kopenick, Czechs from the Sudetenland.

On two previous occasions, Ernst August's reports about Kopenick to Staat had stirred no response, a result he attributed to the continuing jealousy between the Abwehr and the SD. This time, what he offered Staat stimulated commitment to the common cause.

The commitment, or else the irresistible pleasure of wounding the Red network, boosted August over another hurdle with Staat, too. The two men were now sitting outside the Stiftskirche in August's somewhat battered, three-year-old Volkswagen. Staat had wanted to use his chauffeured Mercedes-Benz, but the captain had convinced him of the need for a small car, because to score their coup with Waechter and Kopenick they would likely have to maneuver through the medieval section of the city with its narrow streets and alleys.

They had arrived in the square in front of the Stiftskirche at 1728 hours and were lucky enough to be able to back into a parking space that concealed them from the street. Kopenick appeared at 1729 hours, making August look very good indeed. He stopped in front of the main entrance to the church for about thirty seconds, then drove off.

"Good! Where's the cutout? Why aren't we following?" Staat asked through a thick cloud of cigarette smoke.

"He will be back." It occurred to Ernst for only the first time that Staat probably had no street experience at all. He was just an administrator. "They communicate with their cars," he added.

"Their cars?" Staat was asking questions to which he did not have a ready answer planned. Real questions. Ernst liked that.

"Do you see the little truck across the square? The plumber?" Ernst deliberately pressed on before Staat could answer. He knew the colonel had not noticed the truck. "That's Waechter. He uses different vehicles, but I've seen this one twice before. He also uses a . . . ah, here's Kopenick again!"

Both men watched as the *Rote Kapelle* subagent drove into the square in his tiny, black Renault. This time he did not even stop but drove straight through.

"He's waiting for the traffic to pick up just a bit more," Ernst explained. "The more traffic, the more vehicles, the better for them. But they're running out of time, I think. Waechter can't sit there much longer without attracting attention."

Almost on top of his words, Kopenick reappeared. This time, Waechter pulled out into traffic ahead of him. August accelerated out of the parking space and over the next block slipped the Volkswagen in behind Waechter's truck. Within a few seconds, in what to anyone else would appear to have been natural traffic flow and interchange, the Renault was directly in front of Waechter. The three vehicles moved in single file that way for the next block.

"At the stop ahead," Ernst said. "That's where it'll start."

Staat said nothing but smoked furiously as the line of cars slowed.

"Now! See!" Ernst August could not suppress his excitement. Or his righteousness. "See the message being sent? In Morse! Clumsy, but right in front of our noses! There!"

He translated excitedly.

"Bomb site — No! — *sight* . . . man . . . man . . . must be manufacture — Yes! *manufacture* — moved to Ess . . . Ess . . . *Esslingen*! What did I tell you! 'Bombsight manufacture moved to Esslingen.' They get. . ."

"Hauptmann! They're moving!"

In his excitement, Ernst had almost forgotten he was driving.

"Now wait till we stop again, Herr Oberst, and you'll see more! At this one, perhaps you will read the message for us. I can't stay right behind Waechter too long. He's a careful one!"

Dietrich Staat was exuding extreme discomfort and Hauptmann Ernst August basked in it. He knew the colonel had no idea what was going on.

"What's the matter, Oberst, is it the Morse?"

"Of course not!" the commanding officer snapped. "I know Morse! It's . . . I don't . . . I'm not . . . *How do you know it's Morse?*" The Abwehr captain rolled his window down slightly to let some of the smoke out, then took even more time in an elaborate assessment of whether the ensuing draft caused any discomfort for his superior. Only after he'd stretched the situation to the fringes of bad manners did he reply.

"Under the truck, Oberst Staat. Look under the truck."

► *What has Hauptmann Ernst August discovered? How are Kopenick and Traugott Waechter communicating in Morse code?*

44

THE CASE OF THE MISSING BODY

▼

For some reason, even before she picked up the telephone, Lesley Simpson knew she wasn't going to like this call. Then when the smarmy voice of Eddy Duane greeted her, she knew her instincts had been right on. Eddy Duane was a lawyer in the crown attorney's office. He was not on Lesley Simpson's list of favorite people.

"Hey Les! How are ya?" "Les" would have spoiled the day in any case. Lesley hated being called "Les." Her name was "Lesley," spelled with an E-Y. "The British way," her mother had explained.

"Better brace yourself, Les! We're finally gonna charge your favorite client with murder." That got Lesley's attention. "You see, Les, old kid, we found his wife's body. Well, her skeleton really. It's the late Mrs. Vincent Gene, all right. Absolutely no question. We'll need the dental records to confirm it, but there's no doubt it's her. The ring on the finger, the one earring, the clothes, the shoes. And you know where she was found? Right in the backyard! Your boy's not too bright, Les! Burying his wife in the backyard!"

Suddenly Eddy Duane's voice became more serious. "Look, Lesley," he said. "I'll meet you in, say, an hour or so out at Vincent Gene's house. Cops are there now. The coroner, too. We've agreed to leave everything till you get to see it. One hour. Okay?"

With that, Eddy Duane hung up. Lesley realized she hadn't said a single thing on the telephone other than answering with her own name. Still, conversation wasn't necessary. Not in this case. It was three years old, but Lesley knew every detail as though it had started only yesterday.

Three years ago, the wife of gentleman-farmer Vincent Gene had left her husband sitting at the breakfast table of their expensively renovated Caledon farmhouse and was never seen again. That there had been foul play was pretty certain. Her car was found only minutes away from the house on a barely passable, unmaintained sideroad. It was full of blood — the type matched hers; the front seat had been sliced, presumably with a knife; and a single earring was found on the floor of the passenger side. But her body, if indeed she was dead, had never been found.

Vincent Gene, the husband, was Lesley Simpson's longtime client, and although he insisted he was innocent, the police had focused on him from the beginning. Only the lack of a body, Lesley knew, kept them from laying a murder charge. Now, it seemed, the last hurdle may have been cleared.

It took Lesley only forty minutes to get to Vincent Gene's farm. She noted with relief that Eddy Duane wasn't there yet. Lots of activity though — several police cars, an ambulance, a growing knot of neighbors gathering around the forsythia bushes at the end of the laneway. Near the back of the property, standing beside a backhoe, Lesley recognized Sergeant Rodney Palmer. The recognition was mutual.

"Ah, Ms. Simpson. We've been expecting you," the sergeant said as Lesley approached. Rodney Palmer was as polite as Eddy Duane was pushy. "Over here, if you want to take a look." He took Lesley over to a narrow trench that began where the bucket of the backhoe rested on the ground and ran to a small barn some distance away. Two policemen in coveralls were standing in the trench, their heads just below the top edge.

"It's supposed to be for a water line running to the barn," Palmer said. "They've been digging here four or five days." He nodded at the backhoe. "Operator found the body — uh, the skeleton, rather — first thing this morning. Well, actually, he turned up a shoe first; then when he saw a bone, he stopped and called us. We've almost finished uncovering the whole skeleton now. Wasn't that difficult 'cause the clothes are still in good shape. You want to see?"

Lesley took a deep breath. Then another one. "Yes," she replied.

Rodney Palmer took a few steps and pointed down into the trench without speaking. When Lesley followed and looked down, she knew the sight would stay with her forever. Whatever she had expected, it certainly wasn't color, yet that's what she noticed most of all. Color. The green grass at the top of the trench. Trampled but still green. Then the neat, precise layer of dark brown topsoil. And under that, almost as if someone had drawn a line, a band of yellow. Sand, Lesley figured. Then below that, right to the bottom, blue clay. Maybe it was the blue, she thought, that made the clothing on the skeleton look so, well, so elegantly crimson, dirty as it was.

"See the one earring inside the skull, Les?" The sudden intrusion of Eddy Duane almost made Lesley stumble into the trench. "Quite a sight, huh? One your client never expected to see again, I'll bet. And you know what, it almost worked, too. You see the trench? It was supposed to go over there." He pointed to a spot several yards away. "But there's too much rock, so without even asking, the backhoe guy dug this way and *voilà*! The late Mrs. Vincent Gene. Right in her own backyard!"

Lesley Simpson looked straight at Eddy Duane. "Mrs. Gene," she said, "if indeed that is Mrs. Gene, was not buried here. Not when she died anyway." She shifted her gaze to Sergeant Rodney Palmer. "My guess is that if you can find out who dumped the skeleton into this trench last night and covered it up, you'll have the person who did the killing, too."

► *How does Lesley Simpson know that the skeleton was dumped into the trench last night?*

45

MORE THAN ONE ST. PLOUFFE?

▼

"This is ludicrous. You've got a written confession, written and signed confession, but you've also got two different suspects claiming it's theirs?"

"Yup."

"Two different suspects with exactly the same name?"

"Unnh."

"Alfred-Louis St. Plouffe — *Junior*?"

"Yup."

"And they are father and son?"

"'S right. Father and son."

Struan Ritchie looked up from the confession. "Careful, Kamsack, you almost spoke a whole sentence!"

Effam Kamsack raised both eyebrows in the general direction of his boss and took a deep breath. "Yup," he said again.

Struan waited a second or two just in case there might be

more, but he knew from experience that it was more expedient just to forge ahead.

"Now, just to add to the astounding clarity we are all enjoying in this case, it seems there are actually *three* living Alfred-Louis St. Plouffes," he continued. "Senior, the original; then his son, Junior, and then Junior's son, Alfred-Louis St. Plouffe the Third?"

Kamsack leaned forward again and with his right index finger tapped the report lying in front of Struan. "Yup," he said for the fourth time, and then folded back into a slouch.

"Except that the Third has always called himself Junior also, so in effect there are two Juniors?"

"Unnh."

"So the confession I'm reading here, signed Alfred-Louis St. Plouffe Junior, is claimed by both the Juniors?"

The toothpick in Kamsack's mouth elevated ever so slightly. Struan took that as a "yup." The fifth.

"Well, thank you, Detective Kamsack," he said. "I couldn't have laid it out more clearly myself!"

Kamsack took a while before responding with a grunt, but Struan by then had turned to the source of their mutual interest. The confession was typed on plain white bond paper and signed in a clear, unelaborate script, one that would be simple to forge. The information itself was but three short paragraphs.

On 1 May last, I administered poison in the form of arsenate of lead, to Her Ladyship Teresa Elana Giurgiu, formerly the Countess Covasna of Romania.

Her Ladyship attended mass at St. Sofia's on 1 May, as has been her uninterrupted custom on each of Romania's national holidays since the abdication of King Michael in 1947. During her absence, I added the aforementioned substance to the medicine she consumed three times a day. The effects of the substance, along with all other pertinent details relating to her demise, are known to the police, and I do not dispute their findings or conclusions.

I hereby stipulate that what I have written here is offered of my own free will and without coercion.

Alfred -Louis St. Plouffe Jr.

Alfred-Louis St. Plouffe Jr.

"You know, Kamsack," Struan began, but then stopped abruptly. Kamsack was shifting the toothpick from one side to the other, a sure sign that he was about to volunteer something.

"Got 'em both here for yuh," the detective said very softly. "Think you'll wanna talk to 'em. One a' them's spinnin' yuh 'bout the confession." He slowly undulated to his feet. "Here." He tossed a sheet of paper on Struan's desk. "Ask 'em both these three questions."

Before Struan could react to the longest discourse from Kamsack he could recall in some time, he found himself facing the elder St. Plouffe Junior and, after a few preliminary probes of his own to which the suspect was entirely forthcoming, asked the first of Kamsack's three questions.

"What intrigues us, Monsieur St. Plouffe, is your motive. According to our findings, Lady Giurgiu had very little money . . ."

Alfred-Louis cleared his throat. "Your findings are correct. She had very little money. Indeed, she was nearly destitute, excepting for some ornate jewelry, which I'm convinced she purloined from the royal treasury in 1947."

Struan nodded, using the movement to glance surreptitiously at the second question. "But then, why?" he asked. "She was just a harmless old lady."

193 ◄

"Not harmless when she was younger. Previous to King Michael's abdication, she fabricated a web of intrigue that effectively dissolved our family's fortune. In fact, my family as well. It killed my mother. I can give you the details if —"

"Not just yet," Struan interrupted. "Before we go any further, I have to ask if you are fully aware of the possible consequences of your confession? We have the death penalty in this jurisdiction, you know."

"Yes, I know. But I am not adverse to the idea of death. Not now that I have satisfied the family's honor. And incidentally," St. Plouffe moved to the edge of his chair, "I'm also fully aware that you have to decide between my son and myself as to who is guilty. He foolishly advanced the premise to one of your investigators that it was he who poisoned the Countess. A noble act, but one you should ignore. I did it. The confession is mine."

Struan avoided eye contact with Kamsack while ushering the elder St. Plouffe Junior out of his office and the younger one in. The father and son were remarkably similar in appearance and behavior. In manner of speech too, for to the first of Kamsack's three questions, the one about Lady Giurgiu's financial state, the younger St. Plouffe replied, "Indeed. Unless I have been misled — a distinct possibility, by the way; she was remarkably devious — the Countess Covasna was, how shall I put it, er, impecunious."

"But then, Monsieur St. Plouffe, it's only natural that I ask you *why*." By now Struan had allowed himself to become fascinated with the whole process. "What did you have to gain from poisoning an old lady?"

St. Plouffe's lips curled but didn't quite lift into a smile. "Because of that *old lady's* activities when I was a young child. My health —" He stopped abruptly. "Look, this is superfluous to the matter at hand. I poisoned her. And I am fully cognizant of the potential consequences. Those are the only points about which you need concern yourself. As to my father's attempt to divert you from the truth by claiming authorship of my confession, I can only say that while his gesture is a noble one, it is futile."

Struan stole a quick glance at Kamsack, who was basking in a huge grin. The grin continued long after both St. Plouffes were deposited in the outer office. And it stretched to the limit when Struan said, "My hat's off to you, Effam. Pretty clever. We've got a lot more digging to do on this thing, that's for sure. But at least we know who wrote the confession."

► *Which Alfred-Louis St. Plouffe has written the confession?*

46

NOTHING BETTER THAN
A CLEAR ALIBI

▼

It was not just the old woman's eyes that warned Nik Hall
to go easy; it was the whole package. At Your Peril! was
written all over her.

Beginning with her clothes. The dress, made of satin (or
something equally expensive) was buttoned very carefully
from bottom to top, encasing her like a fortress against all
assaults. The gate was protected by a brooch that was guar-
anteed to be worth more than a month of Nik's salary, and
matched by earrings that, well, he didn't care to speculate.

Even the physical weaknesses that should have betrayed
her years — Nik figured she'd be in her late eighties at least,
but he certainly wasn't prepared to ask — even these weaknesses were subdued, some by subtle means, some by force of
will. An example of the former was the scarf in her lap

that attempted to conceal, ever so casually, hands that were ravaged irremediably by arthritis. The latter was evident in the osteoporosis that had clearly won the battle for her spine but not her spirit, for whatever effort and discomfort it cost her, Augusta Reinhold met Nik's gaze head on. She would not be the one to blink.

It was the eyes that made Nik wish someone else had picked up the telephone an hour ago at the Major Crimes section. So dark and piercing. If the eyes really were windows to the soul, then Augusta Reinhold's had one-way glass.

She spoke first.

"Are you going to stare, detective, or do you want to hear what I have to say?"

Normally, Nik would have blushed, but somehow her question fit the pattern he'd expected. He wanted her to do the talking, and that meant she would have to lead. This was not a lady accustomed to control from outside. The only way into the fortress would be through gates she unlocked herself.

Nik licked his upper lip slowly, then the bottom one, while bringing his fingers together into a steeple. Augusta Reinhold watched him intently, the powerful eyes boring in on his face. He looked back over his left shoulder.

"In the bedroom there," he said, "was your grand-daughter —"

"Who raised you?!"

Nik turned back to the eyes immediately.

"Don't you know enough to look at people when you speak to them?!"

He bowed his head in apology. The gesture let him enjoy a small grin of triumph. He'd confirmed what he suspected: that she was hard of hearing. No hearing aids, though. That would betray weakness.

"Young man." Augusta grabbed the reins with authority.

"Let us get on with this. What you need to know is that my granddaughter was with me when that fool was shot. I won't pretend I'm unhappy he's dead, the parasite, but it was not Siobhan who did the shooting. She is impetuous, I'll grant you. How else could one account for her marrying him so hastily? Marrying him at all! And he abused her terribly. You'll have no difficulty verifying that. But she was out in the hall with me when the shots were fired."

Nik sat expressionless. He already knew that three bullets had brought about the untimely end of Paisley Wendt, and that the noise of three shots had issued from Suite 5 within a minute before or after 11:00 AM. Confirmation of the time had come from two different tenants and the building janitor.

"I was in my solarium having coffee with Esther. That's Esther Goldblum. She's in Suite 14 right across the hall from me. My only neighbor, and a widow like me. We have coffee together every morning when we're in town. Until quarter to eleven. That's when Esther leaves to do her trading. Currencies, mostly. Don't like them. Never have. Too much depends on strange little people thousands of miles away.

"No matter. When Esther left, I went and got dressed as you see me now. On Thursdays I have lunch at the League, you see, and I always take Siobhan. You can verify that easily, too.

"When I got off the elevator here on the third floor, Siobhan was waiting to get on. She was coming to get me, you see. And before you ask, there was no one else on the elevator. It was right then we heard the shots in her suite, and well, the rest is . . . is distasteful, to say the least."

"Mrs. Reinhold." Nik was careful to look straight at her this time. "Do you have a companion or a maid or housekeeper?"

A flicker of wariness crossed the dark eyes.

"Raythena comes in every day at one. She stays as long as is necessary and does what is necessary."

"And how many shots did you say you heard, Mrs. Reinhold?"

The flicker grew to a smolder.

"I didn't say."

"Yes, indeed. Excuse me." Nik spoke very softly. "Er, how many shots do you recall hearing?"

"You think I'm deaf, don't you?" The eyes were sparking now. "That's why you're almost whispering! Well, I'll tell you how many shots I heard. No! First, I'll tell you what you just said. You asked me how many shots I recall hearing, didn't you! I heard three, young man. Three!"

Nik bit down on his lower lip. He took a chance and looked back over his left shoulder again. What he had to decide, and fast, was whether to press harder on Augusta Reinhold to ferret out the truth, or instead to push on the granddaughter. In the end, it was the eyes that helped him decide to go after the younger one. Even if Siobhan was as tough as her grandmother, she had to have softer eyes.

► *What has led Nik Hall to believe that he is not getting the truth from Augusta Reinhold?*

47

THE SEARCH FOR
OLIE JORGENSSON

▼

The instant Detective-Sergeant Connie Mount signaled the little team behind her to halt and take a short break, they all turned to a patch of wild raspberries that grew in profusion at the edge of the trail and began to eat greedily. It was just one more thing that upset her about this search and rescue mission. The searchers were supposed to lie flat and relax totally to conserve their strength; there might be many miles to cover yet and there was plenty of daylight left.

Connie's uneasiness had been growing steadily from the very second this whole affair had started. That was at 7:03 AM this morning, when she walked into the Healey Lake detachment office where she was commanding officer. The night dispatcher, "Lefty" Shaw, still had a half hour left on his shift. He was standing at his desk with his finger on the PLAY button of the answering machine. Connie heard only the very last part of the tape, but she recognized the voice in spite of the panic in it.

". . . don't know how long ago but he isn't anywhere on the campsite! We've looked everywhere! Won't you please hurry! He's so little!"

"That was Svena Jorgensson, wasn't it Norman?" Connie asked.

She was the only one in the detachment — in the entire community — who didn't call him "Lefty"; she felt it kept him on his toes. Police work — his job — became secondary in Lefty's life whenever he was able to lay his hands on a new, or rather, new *old* car. Lefty was a collector of classics and two days ago a 1912 REO had made him completely forget why he was being paid a salary.

"Before you tell me all about it, *Norman*, why is her call on the answering machine instead of on your backup tape? This means you weren't at your desk, were you?"

Lefty's normally ruddy countenance glowed a notch brighter at Connie's challenge. "I had to go to the can!" he said indignantly. "It happens from time to time, you know!"

Connie nodded. "I suppose so. Nature, right?" She took a step forward and pressed REWIND on the answering machine. "You know, that reminds me. It's certainly time those washrooms were cleaned. Especially if we've got to get rid of that Number 90 gear grease you managed to get all over yourself when you were in there."

Lefty turned full red this time but Connie didn't notice. By now she'd punched PLAY and was listening to Svena Jorgensson tell the detachment that her little Olie was missing from their campsite at the lake. As far as she, Svena, knew, he'd gotten up while she was still asleep and wandered off and out into the bush. Olie was only four years old.

That had happened six hours ago, and although Connie had put together a full search and rescue response within forty-five minutes, she still felt that the whole thing might be just a wild goose chase; there were so many things that weren't right to begin with, and so many things that turned out wrong as they went along.

For one, the armed forces helicopter she'd called in to fly over the area with a heat sensor turned out to be a waste of time. There were simply too many wild animals in the area and their body heat made the sensor work like a popcorn machine. The system worked better as the helicopter flew some miles farther from the lake, but there was no point to that because it would have been impossible for a child Olie's age to get that far away in six hours.

The tracking dogs caused another problem. One was a shepherd, the other a Blue Tick hound that Connie had worked with once before. Both dogs led their handlers directly to an abandoned railway line several hundred yards from the Jorgensson's campsite. At that point, the animals disagreed. The shepherd circled and circled and then simply sat down as if to say, "That's it. End of Trail." The Blue Tick bounded down the former railway line in complete confidence, enthusiastically dragging the handler and the search team after him. But then he stopped, too, and like the shepherd, circled a few times and sat down.

By this time, it was 11:00 AM, and the August sun was heating up everyone's nerves, not least Connie's. It was at that point that, against her better judgement, certainly against her best instincts, she let Willy Stefan take over. Not that Willy was incompetent. On the contrary, he was regarded — and rightly so — as the best tracker the area had ever seen. Local wags loved to explain to tourists how Willy could track a mosquito through a swamp. But Willy was not exactly a neutral party in this case. He was Olie's uncle, Svena's brother-in-law, and in the Jorgensson family, that meant complications. Svena and her former husband were involved in a frightfully bitter and ongoing custody dispute over little Olie. That's why Connie had immediately recognized the voice on the answering machine. Olie's father regularly failed to bring him back after "visit" times. Once, the father, with the help of his sister and her husband, Willy, had snatched Olie out of the backyard of the Jorgensson home and had taken him away for two weeks.

These contradictions and complications had been rumbling away in the back of Connie's mind as the search team followed Willy Stefan at a respectable distance down the railway line. Now he stood, after she had called a halt, waiting for her to catch up.

Willy wiped the back of his neck with a peach-colored cloth that said Dunn & Dunn Service. "Slow going," he commented, giving expression to yet another burr that Connie was feeling. They had been moving at a snail's pace all along.

"Tourist season," Willy added as though that explained everything. He held the cloth at the corners and made it flap before wiping his face with it. "There's just so many people hiking along here this time of year," he said through the cloth. "Makes it so hard to read the signs. No wonder the dogs got mixed up."

Connie's reaction was instant. "That does it!"

She turned and yelled back to the others. "You people! I want you to go back a bit. Back up. Go around the curve and wait there till I call."

"Now, Willy," she lowered her voice. "You and I are going to talk. No. Strike that! *You* are going to talk. Talk a lot and talk fast! I want to know where that little boy is!"

▸ *Why does Connie Mount believe that Willy Stefan has something to tell her?*

WHILE LITTLE HARVEY
WATCHED

▼

The starlings came in early the night before Ollie Wicksteed was killed. Little Harvey had watched them from his bedroom window. Black, raucous, a seething, constantly shifting mass that filled the air with ugly croaking. Usually they came in just before sunset but that night they were early, hundreds of them filling up the branches of the old beech tree behind the house.

Grandpa Bottrell said starlings were bad luck. Two years ago, in the fall, the first time Little Harvey remembered them coming in such numbers, Grandpa had taken the old twelve gauge and fired into the tree. It drove the starlings away, but not far and not for long. At the peak of the echoing bang they had risen in an elastic cloud that grew and shrank and shifted above the tree and then simply pulled itself down on the barn roof not far away. Five minutes later they were back in the beech tree and they stayed there, because Momma had taken the shotgun and hidden it. Momma didn't have much patience for behavior like that. It was another one of the things she called "nonsense," a word she used a lot.

Little Harvey rather agreed with her. The shotgun scared him. As for the bad luck part, well, that was different. Grandpa Bottrell always seemed to know about that stuff, and even though Momma called it foolish old peoples' talk, the next day Poppa fell off the ladder out by the implement shed. He was laid up a long time and the neighbors had to finish the ploughing.

It was the next year that Grandpa Bottrell got sick. The same week the starlings showed up. Not as many as the year before — at least Momma said so — but still enough to fill up the old beech tree at sunset and make it impossible to hear anybody talk if you were outside unless they shouted right into your ear. What scared Little Harvey so much was that the day they went away for good that year was the day Grandpa died.

Now they were here again. And Harvey no longer had any doubts about the bad luck. He was in the second grade now and for the first time he was really beginning to like school. This year he didn't even mind the long ride every morning on the old yellow bus. Ms. Caswell was the reason. She was just the best teacher. Every day was fun, but now he couldn't go. The day the starlings arrived Little Harvey had gotten scarlet fever and he had to stay home. Nobody gets scarlet fever these days, Momma had said to Doctor Sannalchuk, and what about the vaccinations when he was a baby? And Doctor Sannalchuk said there were always a very few kids in whom the vaccines didn't "take." Little Harvey had to be one of those. Just bad luck. So he had spent most of a week in his room.

At first he didn't mind, because he was so sick. But by the time Ollie Wicksteed was killed, Little Harvey had felt more like doing things and the starlings at least gave him something to watch. That's why he was looking out the window when Ollie was crushed by the big beech tree. Harvey's room was the only one that faced the back yard.

At the funeral folks said it was an accident and maybe even a blessing, seeing as how Ollie gave his brother such trouble all these years and wasn't really good for anything. Harvey listened to the talk outside the church and he wasn't exactly sure what they meant by "good for anything," but he had a feeling it was because Ollie was funny in the head. People called him retarded but there was a girl in Ollie's class in school who everybody said was retarded and she didn't act the way Ollie did.

Ollie's brother, Carson, was always having to take things out of Ollie's mouth. Once Little Harvey had overheard Poppa say that Carson had had to pull Ollie out of the manure pile at the south barn because he'd tried to burrow in like a groundhog.

"Shame what Carson's had to do for that man these years," Poppa had said. "Every minute he's got to watch. And what does he get for it? His wife leaves him, and you can't blame her after what Ollie done to her that time. Carson, he can't go nowhere. Can't even do a decent day's work. Not much money in firewood no more anyway but a man's got to work. No wonder Carson drinks so heavy."

Momma's response was muffled but Little Harvey was sure he'd heard her mention the special home where Ollie had lived for a time and where he got kicked out and they wouldn't take him back. It was something about a girl there but Harvey didn't know for sure what it was because every time the grown-ups talked about it, they changed the subject when he came near.

It was not only because of the scarlet fever that Harvey was watching from the bedroom window when Carson came over to cut up the beech tree. It was because he was afraid of

Ollie. He didn't used to be, but then Momma had said, "Now the Wicksteed's are neighbors and I don't like to tell you this but you stay away from that Ollie. Don't you dare ever let me catch you makin' fun of him but you stay away."

That's why Little Harvey watched from the safety of the second floor. The night before, a big wind had toppled the old beech, torn it out roots and all, so that it lay tipped on its side like a giant that had fallen with its feet in the air. The hole left by the roots was wide, but because of the way beech trees grow it was shallow, and when Ollie stood upright in it his head was above the surface of the ground. Harvey had watched him rest his chin on the rim of the hole and lick the stones where one edge of the root system still clung to the ground. Then he'd seen Carson turn off the chain saw up at the other end of the tree and throw it down by the branches he'd just cut off and come over and swear at Ollie and kick away the stones. Ollie just sat in the hole for a while after that, but before long he got up onto his knees and began scooping out a burrow with his hands, putting the sandy ground in the pockets of his overalls. That's what he was doing when the stump came down on top of him.

That night the starlings came back at sunset, but they were confused because the beech tree wasn't there. They hovered where the branches used to be as if waiting for them to return, shifting and floating and diving the way they always did. What Little Harvey noticed most of all was how quiet they were. It was as though they knew something. That bothered him a great deal. He knew something too, something about Ollie and the way he died. But who should he tell? And how should he explain it?

► *It would seem that Little Harvey doesn't accept the idea that Ollie Wicksteed's death was an accident. Why has he cause to be suspicious?*

49

A WITNESS
IN THE PARK

▼

At the bottom of the little knoll, Mary Blair paused and looked back at her footprints in the frosty grass. She was grateful she'd decided to wear flats at the last minute. With high heels she would never have been able to walk on the lawn like this for the ground was not yet frozen.

Mary turned a complete 360 degrees. There was no sign of Alicia Bell yet, but that didn't surprise her. It was still too early. She shaded her eyes against the sun as it rose over the top of the knoll, shortening its shadow and shortening hers, too.

Both the public park just to her left, surrounded by an imposing if somewhat ancient iron fence, and the unfenced section of lawn where she was standing had been landscaped years ago into a series of mounds or knolls. None of them were any higher than the average adult, but they gave the impression of rolling terrain, especially from far away. In the park itself, a series of gravel paths and beds of exotic flowers wound their way around the little knolls. Someone had once explained to Mary that the park had been landscaped this way in order to force people to walk through it slowly.

Indeed there was no other park like it in the city. Even its name was impressive: Rousseau Place Botanical Observatory. And it was also unique because it didn't cost the city a cent. Rousseau Place Botanical Observatory was maintained — and very well, too by a pair of wealthy but extremely eccentric flower growers. One of them, Jack Atkin, was Mary Blair's biggest client. The other, Ron Minaker, couldn't be for he was Jack Atkin's arch rival. It was yet another incident in the long-running feud between the two that had brought Mary to the park at a time of day when she preferred to be in bed, or at the very least, dawdling over breakfast. Mary was not an early riser.

"Here I am!" A voice disturbed Mary's reverie. "I say, Ms. Blair, good morning!" A rather stout lady in a tweed suit and an odd Victorian-looking hat was covering the closest knoll at a half trot. "You are Ms. Blair, the lawyer, aren't you? I hope I'm not late, am I? You did say eight o'clock. I had to walk all the way around the park because the gates are locked. They're not opened till ten."

"It's okay. It's okay. You're not late," Mary assured the newcomer. "And yes, I'm Mary Blair. If you know who I am, then you must be Alicia Bell, the witness." She shook Alicia's hand. "Thank you for coming. It's important that we go over what you saw Ron Minaker do before I initiate any formal legal action. You see, you're the only witness, and I want to get a handle on things right here at the scene of the crime so to speak." What Mary Blair did not add was that she also wanted to get a handle on Alicia Bell.

"I understand," Alicia replied. "I've been involved in this

kind of thing before. As a witness, I mean. For Mr. Atkin, too, about ten years ago. It was the time that Mr. Atkin and Mr. Minaker got into that dispute over who had developed a blue azalea."

Mary's eyebrows went up at that one. It had been before her time. She had become Jack Atkin's lawyer five years ago, and in the period since, Atkin had sued Minaker — or vice versa — no less than six times. Every single one of the cases had been thrown out by the trial judge, who then proceeded to scold the two adversaries. And their lawyers! Mary was trying to avoid a repeat embarrassment, which was one of the reasons she had asked Alicia Bell to meet here.

"Now tell me one more time," Mary said, "what it is you saw Mr. Minaker do."

Alicia Bell cleared her throat. "It's quite simple really. As you know, inside the park there are twenty-six flower beds. Mr. Atkin has thirteen. Mr. Minaker has thirteen. The bed over in the far southeast corner is Mr. Atkin's. Has been since they took over the park. Two days ago, in the morning, I saw Mr. Minaker on his knees in that bed. He had a little shovel and he was digging flower bulbs. Digging them *out*, and putting them in a garbage bag."

Mary Blair's voice dropped a few tones as she slid into her cross-examination mode. "You're absolutely sure which flower bed it was?"

"Oh indeed!" was Alicia's reply, "the one in the southeast corner for sure. No doubt about that."

Mary pushed a little harder. "But surely Mr. Minaker saw you, and he wouldn't dig the bulbs out if he knew you were watching."

"Ah, but he couldn't see me!" Alicia Bell's eyes lit up. "Well, he *could* have, I suppose, if he tried real hard. But he didn't. You see, he didn't know I was there. I was behind the knoll in back of the flower bed, something like you and I are right now."

Mary pounced on that one. "But if you're behind one of these knolls, she said, "You can't see what's on the other side!"

Alicia Bell was waiting for it. "Of course not. But I wasn't all the way down at the bottom. More like halfway." She pulled at Mary's elbow and led her up the knoll a few steps. "See? Look! Here we are, only halfway up and you can see everything on the other side. They're only little mounds, these things."

Mary nodded but didn't say anything. She had to admit that it was really quite easy to be concealed and still see *everything* on the other side.

"If you doubt me," Alicia went on, "just wait until we can get into the park, and I'll show you precisely where I was standing. It was a day just like this. Sunny, but a real nip in the air. Leaves falling." She pointed to the frosty grass. "And you could see your tracks in the lawn just like ours here."

Mary nodded again, and again she didn't say anything. But she had heard enough. She was glad she'd got up so early, for she was convinced now that Alicia Bell was a professional witness. A witness available to the highest bidder.

► *What has led Mary Blair to this conviction?*

50

DEATH IN THE
BIDE-A-WEE MOTEL

▼

To Detective First Class Dolores Dexel, the dead man on the floor in front of her was hardly an example of what a big drug operator was supposed to look like. There was no flash to him, no evidence of heavy money, nothing that said "big time." On the contrary, everything about him ranged from mild all the way to even milder.

Starting with the brown slacks. Nothing approaching Italian silk here; these were strictly off the rack. So was the tweed jacket, the kind made to last ten years before leather patches are called upon to adorn the elbows. Dolores couldn't see the shirt or the tie, but she knew what they'd be like. From where she stood, though, she could see the man's sturdy Oxfords had recently been resoled. The heels were new, too; she could read CAT'S PAW semi-circled in the center of each. Even the man's wedding ring said "reliable, ordinary, *solid* citizen." His fingers were curled around the edge of an open Bible — the ultimate touch, Dolores thought — and the ring reflected light from a cheap lamp beside the bed. It was a gold ring, not too wide, not too narrow, no adornment or stones or etched design. Just plain. Solid.

What was most emphatically unordinary, however, was the way he had died. No murder was ever run-of-the-mill, but this one was a step into the unusual. It was an execution. There was a small-caliber bullet wound in the back of the head at close range. Another in the middle of the back and one more at the base of the spine. Insurance shots, Dolores knew. Certainty that the victim was dispatched. The killing shot had been to the front, close range into the heart. At least that's what Dolores thought because of all the blood. She wasn't about to turn him over until the forensic guys got here. She needed photos, too.

That reminded her. What was taking the photographer so long? And the light bar she'd called for? The light especially. The seedy little motel room had a single bedside lamp to supplement the wan glow that tried to reach the floor from the overhead fixture. She needed to be able to see better.

"Forensic just called. They're on their way."

Dolores looked up to see her partner, Paul Provoto, in the doorway. The rattle of the Coke machine just down the hallway was so loud she hadn't heard him approach.

"The lights'll come with the photographer," Paul continued. "And I've got a blue sitting with the night clerk that called in. You can probably talk to her again now. She's not so cranked anymore."

He took a step into the room, then thought better of it. "Gawd. Did this guy bleed or what!"

Paul was right. It was one of the first things Dolores had noted. The blood was not spattered all over as she'd seen so often before (too often — only six months in homicide and already she wanted out). Rather, the blood had flowed — poured! It had run around the outline of the body on the beige tile floor all the way down to the sensible shoes, and in the other direction, along both outstretched arms. It was in the victim's hair (short, getting quite thin. And brown! Dolores had noticed that on the way in). The trail of blood had even curled around the open Bible, as though it were seeking its own path, unhurried, uninterrupted, framing the book neatly so that the double column of text looked even denser from top to bottom. Only the victim's hand, lying on the opposite page, was free of the red substance that was still oozing from the body.

Dolores looked up at Paul. "I'm going to go talk to the clerk," she said. She had to get out of the room. It was suffocating her. "We'll talk in the lobby. Call me if the photographer comes in the back way."

She walked carefully around the body, out past her partner and down the hallway to where the night clerk was waiting. Through the grimy skylight she could see streaks of gray. Be morning soon, she thought. Another night with no sleep.

The night clerk hadn't slept, either, certainly not since she'd called in over an hour ago. For most of the time Dolores and Paul had been at the Bide-a-Wee Motel, the young woman had been drifting back and forth over the border of hysteria.

She was on the calmer side when Dolores entered the lobby, but not comfortably so. She sat scraping away at a gouge in the surface of an end table with an incredibly long, and patently false, thumbnail.

The officer sitting in the only other chair got up. Two chairs, the badly scarred end table, some outdated magazines, and another cheap table lamp made up the "front desk." There was no counter, only a window, a thick Plexiglas one that slid back and forth to enable the duty clerk to accept cash in advance. Nobody used plastic at the Bide-a-Wee Motel.

Dolores sat down gingerly. She didn't want to push the clerk. The chair didn't appear to be up to any serious test, either.

"Miss — " For a second she'd forgotten. "Ah . . . Miss Duvet," she began. "Can you tell me again where you were when you heard the shots?"

The question nearly turned out to be a bad mistake. The night clerk flushed and tears started falling along an already well-worn channel in her makeup.

"I *didn't* hear a shot! I *told* you that! I went for a Coke and I *saw* him . . . the bod —" The tears began to flow faster.

"Yes, yes. That's right. I'm sorry." Dolores put her hand on the young clerk's arm. "Of course you did. My fault."

The soothing tone had effect, and Miss Duvet's tears retreated to snuffles. Dolores also retreated from her ploy to see if the woman's rendering of events had changed since their first encounter.

"Let's go through it one more time." She was going to try a softer tack. "You went down the hall for a Coke. Then what?"

Miss Duvet took a deep breath. It seemed as though she was going to hang together now.

"Then I saw him. The door was — like — open. Like, I mean, who'd leave their door open in a dump like this? And the light's on, too. So I, like, look in. And jeez! There he is!"

"Did you go in?" Dolores took a chance with that.

"No *way*! I mean — jeez! Would *you*? Like — the guy's *dead*! I mean, I *think* he's dead. Like, there's so much blood he's *got* to be dead, right? 'Sides. Even if he's not — like, this ain't Mercy Hospital, right? What do I know from first aid? So I run back here and call 9-1-1. I mean — like — so you're me. What would would *you* do?"

"What time was that?" Dolores asked.

"*I don't know*!" Miss Duvet's fuse was shortening. "I didn't keep track! This ain't a hockey game! They don't even have a crummy clock in here, anyways!"

Dolores noted that Miss Duvet did not wear a watch, either.

"Did you . . ." she decided to go on. "Did you go back to the room then?"

"*Are you nuts*? No way I'm goin' back there! Like, already I gotta full-time picture here. I mean watch this!"

She lifted her face and closed both eyes with emphasis. In the poor light Dolores hadn't noticed till now that Miss Duvet's eyelashes were almost as long as her nails.

"Like, I gotta pair of three-by-fives here. Full-color glossy. You wanna picture? I got it, like every time I close my eyes!"

"It must have been terrible for you." Dolores had decided that the sympathetic approach was definitely going to get better results.

"Terrible. Like — try *mind-blowin'*! I mean, like, this guy. Mr. Straight. Mr. *Brown Clothes*! What's a straight guy like that doin' here, anyways? Like he's even got the Gid out!"

"The 'Gid'?"

"Yeah, the Gid. The Gideon. Like — yuh know — the Bible. He's holding it on one side: 'Gospel according to Matthew.' Like have I gotta picture or *what*? Yuh work in a fleabag like this yuh learn to read upside down. I mean — it's like fun to watch them make up addresses for the reg card. Anyways, I seen the Gid — the Bible. He's got it open. Matthew, right? And the guy's gettin' bald. I seen that, too. I mean I gotta picture. What else yuh wanna know?"

Dolores fumbled in her shoulder bag, ostensibly for a tissue but actually making sure her tape recorder was still running. She was about to ask when Miss Duvet had come on duty, but Paul came in.

"Kodak's here." He pointed out the front door. "And the lighting guys are just pulling in."

Dolores stood. "Tell the photographer to wait," she said. "I want some special shots from the doorway. Also from the feet up." She paused. "And Paul. . . come on out here a minute."

Paul led the way out the door to the parking lot.

Dolores had her notebook out. "I want you to call in some backup teams. Now! As many as the captain will give us for a neighborhood search. And post the blues around the circumference. It's probably too late, but I don't want *anyone* leaving here. Unless Miss Glamorous in there is lying through her teeth, somebody was in that room between the time *she* saw the body and *we* did."

► *Why does Dolores Dexel think that?*

SOLUTIONS
▼

1: THE PROWLER ON BURLEIGH COURT

Inspector Sean Dortmund may well have been unconvinced by Dina White's story because of several small things: Why *three* shots all in the chest if she was so frightened? And how did she get to Lavaliere so quickly? Apparently he was shot right at the window where he came in. The strongest suspicion for Sean, however, is the glass. If Lavaliere had smashed the window and then climbed through, there would not be pieces of glass on *top* of his body. Sean likely believes he was shot first, then the window above his body was broken.

2: DOUBLE SUICIDE ON MIDLAND RIDGE

If the crack between the Jeep door and the frame was covered by masking tape, then the victims were either already asphyxiated by carbon monoxide, or at least unconscious, when they were put in the Jeep. They could not have taped the door in this way if they had been inside.

Jana, if she is the murderer, has unwittingly implicated herself with the note. Even if she is not guilty, she's an obvious suspect.

3: A CLEVER SOLUTION AT THE COUNTY FAIR
The obvious, in the case of homing pigeons: Pincher will take the first-prize ribbon off, and have the judges make their decision again. He will then release the winners of the first prize. Since they are homing pigeons, they will fly home — either to Maxwell Stipple's cote or to Madonna Two Feathers's.

4: A HOLDUP AT THE ADJALA BUILDING
The Adjala Building must function as an almost perfect mirror at almost any time of day, but especially before lunch on this bright day when there would be no direct sunlight on the copper-tinted plate glass doors. The courier quite certainly would have been able to see details about the thief in its reflection.

5: A SURPRISE WITNESS FOR THE HIGHLAND PRESS CASE
In his "favorite" pub, as he claims The Toby Jug to be, Wally Birks is not going to stop at the entrance to the washroom alcove to orient himself on the direction of the "Gents." He'd know which way to turn from habit.

6: THE CASE OF THE MISSING .38 SMITH AND WESSON
It is indeed conceivable that someone could have found a gun in a puddle created by construction. And, as Gary observes, the Smith and Wesson .38 is a fairly common weapon. But the potential suspect's story is flawed from two perspectives:

For one thing, the puddles created by road construction, or any construction for that matter, are rarely filled with clean or even translucent water. Usually it's very dirty, and it would be difficult for anyone to see a gun lying in it (unless he already knew it was there). For another — and this is probably the one that confirms Gary Westlake's suspicions — the puddle is quite likely to be ice-covered, frozen over.

Whoever last used Car 9119 had the fan rear defrost on. A toque, nonregulation, but sometimes used by the highway patrol, was lying on the front seat. The only reason to wear one would be to keep warm. Finally, Gary is wearing gloves. Taken together, the three clues should be sufficient to point to cold winter weather, and ice on still water.

7: A 9-1-1 Call from Whitby Towers

Sandford Verity said that he looked up when he arrived at Whitby Towers to see if Mr. Seneca was watching the incident out on the street. That's when Verity allegedly saw him on the chair, which implies he was about to attempt to hang himself with a nylon rope. However, when Bev Ashby noticed the end of a piece of nylon rope and followed the rope to where it was clamped between the balcony doors, she had to part the drapes with her pen to do so. From the street, Verity could not have seen through the drapes.

8: Before the First Commercial Break

It is too obvious that Katzmann is lying. The allegedly dropped-in-panic revolver is in front of, and against, a door that swings inward (Gilhooley fingers the barrel of the middle hinge). The alleged robber could not have left it like that and then opened the door to flee, because opening the door would have knocked the revolver away.

9: To Catch a Mannerly Thief

Agnes Skeehan walks into her hotel leaning into a strong east wind. She responds to Deputy Commissioner Mowat's phone call and he tells her to go right to the office of the Liverpool CID, specifically to Superintendent Opilis. Through the window of the superintendent's office, Agnes notices a weathervane on a pub across the street pointing right at her. Since the wind is from the east (blowing *toward* the west) the superintendent's office must therefore be on the east side of a street that runs north-south.

Both Agnes and the superintendent then see Alistair Withenshawe across the street, walking toward the police station because he was summoned there. Opilis told Agnes that Withenshawe Purveyors has an office just a short walk to the south. Therefore, this "dude," as Agnes called him, is walking toward the north, on the west side of the street. His cane must be in his street-side hand, or *right* hand, for he first bounces it off the curb, then twirls it over parked cars.

Agnes concludes that to engage in such adept cane work, Alistair Withenshawe must be using his preferred hand, his right hand, the same hand he would use to write notes. Since the jewel thief's notes are written by a left-handed person, Agnes is willing to give odds that Withenshawe didn't write them.

10: SOMETHING SUSPICIOUS IN THE HARBOR
On this second trip to the big freighter, Sue was able to see from her rowboat the paint scrape, where that morning the police boat had bumped into the side. Yet the *Christopher Thomas* had been receiving heavy cargo for several hours before the first visit, it was being loaded all day, and it was still being loaded when she made her unofficial trip. A freighter receiving cargo like this settles into the water as it is being loaded. Therefore, Sue should not have been able to see the paint scrape from the morning visit. By now, it should have been under water. Tomorrow morning she is going to have a careful look at the cargo, probably to see whether it is

really automobile engines, or maybe to see if there is any cargo at all.

11: Esty Wills Prepares for a Business Trip

Sean wears an overcoat and there is snow, so it's winter in Chicago. While Paraguay's climate may not be well known (it's generally tropical), what is well known is that the country is situated below the equator, and therefore it's summer there. That being the case, why is Wills packing a scarf, gloves, and wool socks?

Incidentally, Japan did undertake a mulberry bush experiment in the 1980s for silk production. It continues.

Flying time, Chicago to Buenos Aires via commercial airlines, is about sixteen hours. Flying to Asunción adds two hours for time-zone changes.

12: The Power of Chance

In all likelihood, Walter "Whispering" Hope has impaired hearing. He speaks very loudly, which is typical of people with diminished hearing capacity. Still, this may just be habit from trying to communicate on construction sites. The clincher is seeing Hope at work on a backhoe without hearing protection. It's very likely he has hearing damage if that's the way he works.

There is another element that may also prove to be pertinent. Whether Tom knows it or not (he'll certainly discover it if he looks into Walter Hope) on most construction sites the workers wear yellow hard hats and the bosses wear white ones. If Hope is a bossman, he's likely been around these noisy places for some time.

If it's going to be Hope's testimony that he overheard the defendants trying to deal goods on the patio of a bar, which itself is not an acoustically ideal location, there is good reason to suspect his credibility as a witness.

13: An Unlikely Place to Die

The time of day is early morning because Brad got trapped in rush-hour traffic. The gardener discovered Mme de Bouvère's body just after sunrise and turned on the alarm. The coroner estimates the time of death at between 10:00 and 11:00 the night before. Therefore, if Mme de Bouvère and the man lying outside the gazebo had gone out to play tennis and indulge in some drugs the evening before, they would have walked over the lawn that surrounded the gazebo while it was still wet or at least damp from the rain that accompanied the late afternoon thunderstorm the day before. Because the gardener cuts the lawn every second day, and because he cut it yesterday, *before* they walked to the gazebo, Mme de Bouvère would surely have picked up a blade of grass (likely several) on her white sneakers. Yet Brad noticed that her sneakers, like the rest of her clothing, were pristine: entirely free of any specks. It appears to him that she somehow got to the gazebo without making contact with the lawn. Whether or not she died of a drug overdose, it is likely that someone carried her there after she was already dead.

14: The Last Will and Testament of Norville Dobbs, Orthographer

Amy was acutely aware of Norville Dobbs' obsession with accurate spelling. He would never have signed a document that spelled *supersede* incorrectly.

15: Not Your Average Hardware Store

In a hardware store where customers can buy "real" hardware from bins and barrels and shelves, where things are not prepackaged in a cosmetic sort of way, the clerks get dirty hands, for obvious reasons. Over time, the hands naturally become somewhat marked by years of digging into barrels of oil-covered nails and shelves of greasy bolts. This victim had a soft white hand showing in the small of his back. Therefore, it surely is not Wilfrid Norman, a longtime hardware store owner.

16: WHO HID THE MEDICINE?

Val Horst carries a white cane signaling to the rest of the world that he is blind. Yet Christian noted that Val Horst knew what Harry the twin had communicated in sign, about being in his room with his brother all the time. Christian, quite rightly, wants to find out why Val Horst is pretending to be blind. In that may be the answer to the hidden medication.

17: SHOULD THE THIRD SECRETARY SIGN?

Probably not, for the photograph is fraudulent. Russia uses the Cyrillic alphabet, in which the letters of Lenin's name, most particularly the "L" and "I," bear no resemblance at all to those letters as we know them in the modern Roman alphabet.

The Cyrillic alphabet, modified from Greek by St. Cyril (c. 827–869), is used for Slavonic languages like Russian and Bulgarian. As Third Secretary, Ena would surely have known that, and likely would have declined to sign.

When the USSR moved into Czechoslovakia on August 21, 1968, Austria became the first stop for most refugees.

Lenin died in 1924. In 1930 his tomb was built in Red Square, with his embalmed body visible behind glass. It became a type of shrine in Moscow but was removed after perestroika.

18: THE CASE OF THE JEWELRY THIEVES

When Steve Fleck picked up the young lady at the bus stop, it was at least 6:00 PM. He had been in the car for two hours, since the robbery at 4:00 PM. In what is obviously a northern-hemisphere climate one week before Christmas, darkness would have fallen at least an hour before; therefore, the young lady could not have seen that the passing Japanese car was blue; even noting a dented fender was unlikely. Steve suspects she is a plant, to convince him that the thieves have headed east out of Lindeville.

19: THE MURDER OF MR. NORBERT GRAY

The letters in the evidence bag are personal ones, mailed by someone. Mike Roslin tapped the stamps on both letters, so it is likely that whoever mailed the letters licked the stamps.

The saliva can be tested for DNA.

20: SOME UNCERTAINTY ABOUT THE CALL AT 291 BRISTOL

1) Shaun's maternal instincts are readily apparent, so it must seem strange, at the very least, that Paige's parents would go away, leaving her alone in the house, with the burglar alarm not working, especially given the recent stalking incident on the campus.

2) If the man in black was breaking and entering, it seems highly unlikely he would wear jewelry that might jingle.

3) The strongest doubt of all originates from Paige herself. If she had just emerged from the shower, the mirror in which she claims to have seen the man in black would have been fogged with vapor.

21: THE CASE OF THE STOLEN STAMP COLLECTION

Miles Bender described one of the "police officers" as having blue eyes and a reddish moustache. He also said the officers had real uniforms and genuinely appeared to be motorcycle police personnel, complete with the sunglasses they typically wear. But if they had sunglasses on, how would Miles Bender have known the eye color of the one who got close to him?

22: THE CASE OF THE BUCKLE FILE

Gibraltar is spelled Gibralter in both the letter from Audrey and the one from Irene. The coincidence is too strong for Christine Cooper, who feels that Audrey, whose body, unlike that of Ernie, was never found, may be involved in a scheme to collect insurance. Irene's (Audrey's?) mistake is that she misspells Gibraltar even though, supposedly, she has been living there.

23: A VERY BRIEF NON-INTERVIEW

When Sheila Lacroix entered the office, the office door was behind her, and the wall to her left held books and news-papers. Ahead of her (the third wall) was glass through which she could see central Amman. On the remaining wall, Ibrahim Jamaa, or rather, his substitute, was signing documents.

He had his back to Sheila and he was covered with *thobe* and *aba* so that only one hand was exposed. Since the hand rested on the back of his hip and the index finger pointed to the windowed wall, the hand therefore must have been his right. He was signing documents with his left hand, and so he must be left-handed.

When Ibrahim Jamaa's substitute took two steps to the edge of his desk and spoke to Sheila, he ran one of his long index fingers over the shoulder cradle of the telephone and along the thin neck of a desk lamp. For a left-handed person, those items are on the wrong side of the desk.

If he prefers to speak on the telephone and write while doing so (hence the shoulder cradle), the telephone would be on the other side of the desk so that the receiver could rest on his right shoulder while he wrote with his left hand. If there is any doubt about this logic, it is dispelled by the position of the desk lamp. It's on the same, or wrong, side of the desk.

24: A CLEAN PLACE TO MAKE AN END OF IT

One of the very clear pieces of evidence is that the body has been dead for some time. The odor makes that certain, so it is quite likely that, as the coroner says, the victim has been dead for forty to fifty hours.

Therefore, if the woman backed the car into the garage that long ago, and left the motor running until she died, the car would have run out of fuel, and the battery would have been drained to powerlessness owing to the fact that the ignition was left on. Yet Bob was able to lower one of the windows by simply ticking the switch. He suspects that this car may not be the place where the person died.

25: MURDER AT THE DAVID WINKLER HOUSE

Chris Beadle walked into the tiny washroom pushing the door open wide. The door barely cleared the sink in the corner ahead and to the left. The sampler is hanging on the wall behind this door. If Kate Mistoe had been nailing up this sampler when the shots were fired, she would have had to close the door. Otherwise she would not have been able to get at the wall.

The problem with her alibi arises out of the fact that Sandy Sanchez says he saw her as he passed, at the time the shots were fired. (They stared at each other in shock and fear.) If the door had been closed, he obviously would not have seen her.

When Sandy spoke to Chris and animatedly made clockwise motions with his fist to describe the tightening of the fitting on the propane system, he may have been inadvertently revealing ignorance about propane systems. Threaded fittings throughout the world are tightened clockwise and loosened counterclockwise. By international agreement, threaded fittings used in gas systems (e.g., propane) are tightened and loosened in the opposite way.

Karl Schloss had the oil changed in his car. The service station would have noted the odometer reading at the time of this oil change. By checking the odometer reading right now, Chris can calculate how far he drove after leaving the service station. By having him retrace the route he said he covered on the way back to Winkler House, Chris would be able to verify whether or not he actually did so.

26: A QUIET NIGHT WITH DANIELLE STEEL?

The platform jutting out from the side of the Jacuzzi is completely clean. If the victim had taken a novel and a drink to the tub, and if the drink was almost entirely consumed, then the glass would have been lifted up and set down several times, leaving round marks on the surface of the platform. If she died of natural causes and then sank into the water, taking the novel in with her, those marks would still be there. Even an obsessively neat woman would not have wiped them after each sip. (Besides, the only cloth, the face cloth, was untouched.) Someone must have cleaned too thoroughly in an attempt to rid the place of evidence.

27: RIGHT OVER THE EDGE OF OLD BALDY

When Pam heard the scream, she was only a minute or so away from the edge of Old Baldy. She had been proceeding up the Bruce Trail from Kimberley Rock. Hadley Withrop said that he and Sheena had eaten lunch at Kimberley Rock and had been at the edge of Old Baldy for only two minutes when Sheena went over. If this account is true, then the Withrops had gone up the trail just ahead of Pam. By the same token, if that fact is true, the Withrops would have taken out the spiderweb that Pam ran into. There would not have been sufficient time for the spider to rebuild. If the Withrops had not come up the trail ahead of Pam, why does he say that?

28: The Case of Queen Isabella's Gift

Even though the vicar is a clear suspect, his story that a visitor to Evensong hid in the church is entirely plausible. But the story breaks down over the electric lights. Geoffrey's visit to St. Dunstan's-by-the-Water takes place during the day. Chief Inspector Peddelley-Spens, during his tirade, said that the prime minister of Portugal was coming in "this afternoon" and that he wanted Geoff back "before tea." It took Geoff an hour to get to St. Dunstan's, so it is daylight when he and the vicar enter the church.

They unlock the main door and enter. The church is dark and the vicar turns on the lights, so lighting is necessary at all times, even daytime, to function in the church. Because the vicar asks Geoff to exit by the main door so they can turn the lights out and lock up, the only light switches must be at that door.

If the vicar entered that morning by the back emergency door (as usual) and looked up (which was unusual), would he have been able to see that the candelabra were missing without first going to the back of the church and turning on the lights? The candelabra, after all, were placed so high that even with a step stool and an extended candlelighter they were difficult to light. It is far more likely that the vicar already knew they were missing.

It is interesting to note that Geoffrey was also very much aware that the conflict between Edward II and his queen, Isabella, was so intense that by 1326, six years after the dedication of St. Dunstan's, it had degenerated into civil war or, depending on one's point of view, a legitimate revolution. It's quite possible that in 1320 they may not have attended a dedication together.

George IV became Prince Regent in 1810. His father, by this time, was reported to be having animated conversations with a tree in the Great Park at Windsor, thinking it was Frederick the Great.

29: Murder at 249 Hanover Street

The butler is the only one with a careless alibi. He said he went to his sister's in Kennebunkport on the 30th for two days. Even though his sister may prevaricate on his behalf, he has still made the mistake of saying the "30th." The day is October 1 (as the radio announcer said), so if he was in Kennebunkport for two days, he could not have gone there on September 30. There are only thirty days in September.

30: Waiting Out the Rain

While Michelle sat at Kline's Soda Shoppe with her friends from Memorial Junior School, she watched a little boy standing in the gutter, enjoying the rainfall. He had boots on and the runoff was rushing up against the toes of the boots. This is confirmed by the candy wrapper which flowed up to his toes and then floated between the boots. The flow of the water therefore defines the slope of the street.

Behind the little boy (and downstream) is a woman, quite likely his mother. She is standing at Whippany Appliances, next door to Kline's, listening to the news about the D-Day landing in France.

When Michelle and Julie leave Kline's, they walk past Whippany Appliances and see the two men unloading a truck belonging to Bitnik's Delivery Service. The truck is still further "downstream" from Kline's. If its emergency brake failed, it would not have rolled toward Kline's Soda Shoppe, but the other way. To cause the damage it did, the truck would have had to smash into Kline's window while under power. It was obviously not an accident.

31: The Body on Blanchard Beach

Dexter Treble explained that although the tire tracks were clear and preserved, there were no footprints. Had the body been brought to Blanchard Beach in the trunk of a car, or the back of a pickup truck, the deliverer would have had to get out of the car and walk around to the back to remove the body.

32: THE CASE OF THE MISSING CHILD

While standing in the doorway, Audrey noticed that, behind the father, the venetian blinds are open. At the other window, the mother is looking out. Both say they have not been in the room since Lexie was put to bed last night. In a bedroom exposed to higher buildings such as the neighboring apartments, it surely would have been natural to draw the blinds. This is especially so in light of the mother's statement that anything, including light, can set Lexie off. It seems the parents have much more explaining to do.

33: THE CASE OF THE ATTEMPTED SUICIDE

Berenice Devone is unquestionably a sophisticated and experienced hostess who, while pouring tea, is in her element. Yet she had committed an unpardonable social gaffe by pouring tea for Jasmine Peak without first asking her how she would like it served. She would only do this if the two knew one another or had been together for tea before. Yet they supposedly, except for a stressful encounter at the hospital, had never met!

34: THE MISSION IN THE CLEARING

In the days before blood packs and refrigerated plasma supplies, or in conditions where these things were unavailable, it was not unusual to transfuse directly from one person to another in an emergency. Since Haight-Windsor is O-negative, the surviving priest will be able to receive his blood, because O-negative is a universal donor, as Ron Forrester says. (Other factors of course, would be taken into account in a modern hospital, but that's not where this is happening!)

Throckton believes that with enough blood, Haight-

Windsor's and Ron's — if it's the right type — he can keep the priest alive until they get to the airstrip. The question is this: is the priest A-positive like Ron?

Using the following reasoning, he is, and given the emergency and the fact that he is *in extremis*, anyway, it's the best they have. Of the two priests who were bound together, the one on the left is somewhat unkempt and disheveled. He is the one who is alive (his Roman collar was dirty) and also the one whose right shoe is scuffed at the heel from top to bottom. That's the kind of scuff a right shoe gets if it is worn by a vehicle driver. The heel wears from the rotation at the accelerator. This particular priest must be the one who drives the mission's pickup truck then, and it must be his blood type disk (A+) on the ring with the ignition key.

35: In Search of Answers

It is understandable that Celeste would be suspicious of Virgil Powys. After all, he has been having difficulties with his freelance business, so a cleverly arranged theft might make it possible for him to garner two or even more fees for Hygiolic's medical discovery. But Celeste needs more than suspicion; she needs good grounds for suspecting that Powys intended to be out of the studio longer than the ten or eleven minutes he claims.

Her suspicions arise out of what she observed on the reproduction Chippendale table. The weather has been very hot so all the windows are wide open. Even though Powys's studio has windows on three walls and is on the second floor (or is, at least, elevated), there is still no movement of air for there is no breeze.

Why, then, would someone who intends to be out for only about five or six minutes (he didn't know he was going to get a phone call — or did he?) place a heavy metal stapler on his working papers unless he expected that they might be blown around? And they would be blown around only if a wind were to rise. Given the conditions at the time Powys left the studio, this was not going to be an immediate possibility, or at least not a possibility in five or six minutes. Powys apparently intended to be out of the studio for longer than he claimed, which, in Celeste's opinion, is worth probing further.

36: Vandalism at the Bel Monte Gallery

While Robbie paced on the sidewalk, waiting for Patchy, Dale stood between the sidewalk and the Bel Monte Gallery, under a mature chestnut tree. The time is just before Christmas, and there would not be any leaves on the tree. Four months ago, when the paintings were slashed, the tree would have been in full leaf. That it is a chestnut tree is not overly significant; however, the leaves of this type of tree are very large and the tree always leafs very fully.

From the bus shelter, Patchy draws the attention of the two investigators to the window "right b'tween them branches there." His ability to "witness" would almost certainly have been thwarted by the leaves at that time.

37: Two Shots Were Fired

Because of the heat wave, it is reasonable to believe that the door was indeed propped open as the guard said. And it may well be that the guard faced the front if that's where previous break-ins occurred. Therefore, his back would have been to the open door. However, even though the open door faced east, and what would therefore have been the rising sun, the fact is there was no rising sun at the time of the shooting. The area was covered with gray cloud when the shooting took place, between 6:00 AM and 7:00 AM. (When Vince Pogor arrived, it was noon and the crime was already six hours old.) The sun did not come out until Vince was driving to Toronto, some time after he was about to listen to the 8:00 news while eating his breakfast.

Given these conditions, the security guard's statement that he was startled by a dark *shadow* from the doorway behind him is highly suspect.

38: INVESTIGATING THE FAILED DRUG BUST

Officer Dana is already under quiet investigation; that is a given. The second officer to be checked out now is the narcotics squad officer from Gallenkirk Park. He is the one who said that the approaching wino (Officer Dana) could be heard walking through the leaves.

Quite clearly, the time is early spring. There is some snow still remaining in shaded spots and in the lee of tree trunks. Betty Stadler is sure she noticed a robin and remarks that it is an early returner. In early spring, the millions of leaves that fell from the many trees in Gallenkirk Park the previous fall will be soggy and compressed and matted together. This would have been especially so at the time of the failed drug bust and during Betty's subsequent investigation because the effect of the melted snow has been compounded by several days of drizzle.

For Officer Dana to have made noise walking through the leaves, he would have had to stir up the surface very deliberately, implying some connection to the meeting of drug dealers about to take place. Another possibility is that the narcotics officer is not telling the truth about the way Officer Dana approached. Still a third is that the two officers are in this together. Thus, for the moment at least, Lieutenant Stadler has two police officers to investigate.

39: A DOUBLE ASSASSINATION AT "THE FALLS"

The two diplomats were of significantly different height. One was about the height of the sergeant, who is a head taller than Vince. The other was about Vince's height.

When Vince sat in the driver's seat of the car, waiting for clearance to tow it away, he adjusted the rearview mirror *down* so he could see out the back. Therefore it must have been adjusted for a taller person before: the taller of the two diplomats.

40: A Decision at Rattlesnake Point

Without doubt, Perry Provato will examine the body at the morgue, looking for possible causes of death other than trauma from the two-hundred-foot drop. Trevor, however, has drawn some preliminary conclusions because of the size of the dead person and the position of the steering column.

From Perry's and Trevor's observations, it is clear that the dead person is big. Most particularly, he has a very big belly. If he had driven the Lincoln Town Car to the edge of Rattlesnake Point, parked it, and then jumped over in an apparent suicide, he would surely have tilted up the steering column and wheel in order to get out of the car. This is automatic behavior in large people whose cars have this feature (as all newer model luxury cars do). The fact that Trevor had to tilt up the steering column in order to get his own large frame in to peer under the seat suggests to him that someone else drove the car to Rattlesnake Point. That can only mean the victim was already dead when the car was parked there, or that he was thrown over the cliff

This conclusion may or may not be strengthened when Ashlynne checks the pre-set radio stations. The owner surely prefers country music. If when she turns the radio on, it is not tuned to a country station, that would reinforce the contention that the driver was someone other than the owner. If the pre-set stations do not include country music stations, this may suggest further discrepancy.

Why the car was parked so carefully and locked is an issue.

However, the open trunk revealed the neatness with which the vehicle was kept, likely a characteristic of the victim. It is probable that Trevor's investigation of "A." will reveal that he was an orderly person. The murderer, no doubt aware of that, must have deliberately parked and locked the car in the way that A. would have done.

41: WHEN THE OXYGEN RAN OUT

Either there is a series of genuine and unfortunate coincidences or there is a conspiracy that has led to the death of Humbert Latham.

The day nurse may have left innocently; after all, she had arranged to leave early. The valet's accident may have been real, along with the subsequent wooziness and inability to speak. As for the night nurse, we don't know why she failed to show up, but if the other two were legitimately absent, she could have been too. On the other hand, if there is a conspiracy by one or two or all three of the above, the security guard, if he was the regular patroller, would likely have been part of it.

Fran noted that the lamp was on in the room with Latham's body. If, as Sergeant Hong ordered, nothing was to be touched, then it must have been on all night. Since there was no blind or curtain over the window, the regular patroller would have noted the light, and unless he was in on a plot, would surely have investigated.

42: THE CASE OF THE SCALPEL MURDER

Although the initial evidence may suggest that Doc Virgil killed Petty in the car while he was drunk and then crawled into the back seat to sleep, Gary is suspicious of the obviousness of this.

It is likely that Gary believes someone else killed Petty while Doc was passed out, and then drove the car containing her body and Doc, to the spot on the Fourth Concession where it was found.

His first suspicion is the chocolate-bar wrapper. Is Doc, with his obsessive nature and his concerns for diet, going to eat a candy bar? Petty was not likely to, since she was a diabetic.

Secondly, Doc Virgil was a little man; yet Gary had to move the front seat ahead to reach the pedals.

Finally, when the car had been turned off, the radio was not tuned to an all-country station.

43: SPY VERSUS SPY

Because the *Rote Kapelle* did not use radios in Stuttgart to any great extent (at least in our story) the counterespionage service of German intelligence did not have great success with the direction-finding equipment used to locate clandestine radios — and thereby spies — in World War II. It is reasonable to assume, therefore, that Kopenick is not sending Morse code messages to Traugott Waechter by means of special equipment they have had installed in their vehicles. (Besides, Waechter shows up in a variety of vehicles; that would have been too much of a technical challenge had they been using such equipment.)

For obvious reasons, they would not be communicating with written signs or hand signals, not in the midst of traffic in a German city in the middle of World War II.

Then there's the fact that Hauptmann August can read the code while he is *behind* Waechter's little truck and cannot see Kopenick at all. The only way that the Morse can be used, therefore, is through the brake lights. When the vehicle stops (Kopenick's) he taps out the code to Waechter right behind him. Ernst August told Oberst Staat they had to see the two spies rendezvous while it was still raining. Either by luck or persistence, August had no doubt learned that by driving behind Waechter when the pavement was wet, he could see the brake lights of the car in front (Kopenick's) reflected off the pavement beneath the following vehicle (Waechter's). By that means August could see and translate the Morse message.

This apparently naive method of communication (Ernst August called it "clumsy") was actually used from time to time, especially in World War II. It is highly likely that real spies would not have communicated in open Morse, however, but would have had a code developed for the purpose.

The use of Morse code had declined dramatically by World War II in favor of the far more economical Baudot Code devised by a French engineer (named Baudot, what else!) in 1874. Still, who has ever heard of Baudot Code?

The *Rote Kapelle* was exceptionally successful as a Soviet network in the early years of the war, but careless use of their radios, along with increasing sophistication in radio location techniques and technology on the part of German intelligence, reduced their effectiveness by 1943. Post-war analysis, incidentally, attributes the networks downfall largely to the fact that too many agents knew one another. They did not use "cutouts" sufficiently or effectively so that when one was caught, the domino effect was very damaging.

44: THE CASE OF THE MISSING BODY

Lesley Simpson could see that at the point in the trench where the skeleton was found, the earth was being excavated for the very first time as the trench was being dug. Had someone buried the body of Mrs. Vincent Gene there three years ago, the earth would have been disturbed by that excavation. However, what Sergeant Palmer pointed out to Lesley was a skeleton lying in earth that was still in its natural layers. It is entirely likely that this earth hadn't been disturbed since the last glacier passed through.

Therefore, the skeleton of Mrs. Gene must have been brought to the trench from elsewhere, dropped in, and then covered with loose earth for the backhoe operator to find the next day. If Vincent Gene is charged, it will likely be Lesley Simpson's argument that he is being framed by someone who put the body in the trench in an attempt to make it appear as though she had been buried there some time before.

45: MORE THAN ONE ST. PLOUFFE?

Alfred-Louis St. Plouffe Junior *fils*.

The confession is written in grammatically impeccable prose. The same quality applies to the speech of the younger St. Plouffe Junior. The speech of the elder St. Plouffe Junior, however, while grammatically elegant for the most part, has some awkward errors, suggesting he does not have quite the grammatical exactitude necessary to write the confession in the way it was offered.

The elder St. Plouffe says *adverse* when *averse* is the correct choice, and *previous* instead of *prior*. Further, he says *between my son and myself*, a very popular vulgarism, instead of *between my son and me*. The use of *excepting* over *except* is another grammatical sin.

46: NOTHING BETTER THAN A CLEAR ALIBI

Only Augusta and Siobhan can support the contention that they were in the hallway when the three shots were fired that apparently killed Siobhan's husband, Paisley. Everything else can be attested to by other tenants, the janitor, and Esther Goldblum.

Where Augusta Reinhold's account breaks down, and what makes Nik Hall suspicious of Siobhan's alibi, is Augusta's statement that after Esther left, she got dressed "as you see me now" and came down the elevator to Siobhan's floor. Nik realizes that without the help of Raythena, who does not appear until 1:00, Augusta would never have been able to button the dress she has on, in the space of time described, because her hands are ravaged by arthritis. She could never have made it to the elevator and be in it with her granddaughter within the time she claims.

47: THE SEARCH FOR OLIE JORGENSSON

Willy Stefan, as Connie knew, is not a neutral party in this case, being Olie's uncle, Svena's brother-in-law, and perhaps most important, being married to the sister of Olie's father.

Willy has been leading the search team down the abandoned railway line at a very slow pace. He explained to Connie that the slowness was owing to the fact that signs along the trail were hard to read, there being so many tourists hiking down the line at this time of year. His mistake was in giving that as his excuse. If there were enough tourists walking along this line to disrupt the tracking process, those same hikers would have cleaned out the wild raspberries, too. Yet they grew in abundance at the edge of the trail. For reasons that Connie wants to uncover, Willy has lied to her.

48: WHILE LITTLE HARVEY WATCHED

Carson Wicksteed, according to Harvey's parents, has had a difficult time because of his brother. To some people, that would imply motive. Carson must also know what he's doing with a chain saw, especially if he's been making a living out of firewood as Little Harvey's father says.

The beech tree fell over intact during the storm, its roots still attached to the tree and, at one edge, still clinging to the ground. Unless a sawyer is deliberately trying to make the stump fall back into the hole, he will not cut away the upper part of the tree first, because it is the counterbalancing weight of the upper part that keeps the stump and root system from doing so. Since Carson is a professional, he would surely have known this.

49: A WITNESS IN THE PARK

The season must be autumn, for Mary Blair's shoes leave prints in the frosty grass. Alicia Bell says there are leaves falling. Yet it must still be early autumn, for Mary notes that the ground was still too soft to walk on in high heels.

Anyone who gets up early enough on crisp but sunny autumn days, when the temperature is close to freezing, has seen the frost on the grass sparkling in the sunlight. However, particularly in early fall, that sparkle disappears within two to three hours of sunrise at the latest as the earth warms.

Alicia Bell was doing fine with her story about Ron Minaker digging flower bulbs out of Jack Atkin's flower bed until she mentioned the footprints in the frosty grass. It's quite possible that two days ago when the alleged digging took place, the weather was identical to the weather on the day Mary and Alicia met. And it's quite possible that Alicia could have been concealed just over the brow of a knoll behind the flower bed in question. But she couldn't have stood there until at least 10:00 for the park gates are locked until then. By that time, in early fall, the frost on the grass has long melted away in the sunlight.

It appears that Alicia Bell was enjoying her story so much that she went too far.

50: DEATH IN THE BIDE-A-WEE MOTEL

Dolores Dexel feels that the scene has been tampered with and that the person(s) who did it may still be around. Her deductions are based on the circumstances of the Gideon Bible. From where she stood at the victim's feet (she could read the brand name on his new heels) she was looking along the body and out to the doorway. And from that perspective she could see the victim's left hand (the wedding ring) grasping the edge of the book, with the palm over the page. On the uncovered page, Dolores could see a double column of text top to bottom.

Miss Duvet reported that in her "picture," she could see the Bible open to the "Gospel according to Matthew." Since she did not go into the room, Miss Duvet must have read that from the hallway or at best from the doorway. In this case, with the poor lighting, the only type large enough to actually read would have been the type from a title page.

A title page always appears on the *recto* (right-hand) side of a book. That's the way a book is laid out for printing. For an important or main title, or one indicating a major change in contents, it would be exceedingly rare to find it on the left or *verso* page. Matthew is the first of the four gospels of the New Testament — a major change in contents — and a Bible with the title page to the Matthew gospel on the left would be an extremely unusual one.

What all this means is that if Dolores saw a double column of text top to bottom on the exposed page when she was in the motel room with the body, then the title page (on the recto or right-hand side) is covered by the victim's hand. And the book, in that case, is turned *toward* the doorway. When Miss Duvet said she read "Gospel according to Matthew" upside down, it means the book was turned *away* from the doorway at the time. The recto side, the one with the title, would have been the uncovered page if this were the case.

Dolores is taking the position that Miss Duvet is telling the truth. There's no reason for her to have falsely added the bit about reading the title page upside down.

Finally, Dolores's deductions have determined that if someone moved the Bible, it must have happened fairly soon after the killing, because when she came to the scene the blood had framed the book neatly. It had flowed around after the book was moved; there would have been smudging otherwise. (It also means that Miss Duvet came upon the scene very shortly after the man was killed, which is why Dolores would like to know more about the time when she called.)